Finding Noah

FOGGY BASIN SEASON 2

GABBI GREY

Noah

I need a fresh start, and Foggy Basin, California, is the perfect place to begin my new life. The accepting small town is such a contrast to the large town I came from. Making a success of my dog-training business—Tricks, Tips, and Backflips—is important to me, and I totally lucked out when my straight best friend, Christian, decided to move with me. He makes my life easier. I just hope he'll be as happy here as I am.

Christian

Following my best friend to Foggy Basin was a no-brainer. I've been in love with him since we were five years old. Problem is, I've never had the guts to say so, and while he's out and proud, I'm still in the closet. Somehow, I need to find the courage to make a move before he finds someone else in this gay-friendly town, but Noah thinks I'm straight, and I'm not sure what he'll do when I tell him that's not exactly true.

Finding Noah is a 44k small-town, friends-to-lovers, interracial, gay romance with fresh starts, well-meaning but nosy neighbors, and some special critters who are along for the ride.

Welcome to Foggy Basin, Season Two. Just passing through? No problem. Here to stay? Well, better find your place. Sit back, relax, and get to know the townsfolk. They love hard and play even harder. Each book is a standalone, but why not stay and get to know us and read them all?

multimedia, audio, or other medium. We support the right of humans to control their artistic works.

No generative AI was used in the creation of this book.

Edits by ELF

Cover by BL Maxwell

Dedication

Jeanine – thank you for your friendship

Contents

Prologue

Noah

I stared at the photographs in my hands, not quite believe what I was seeing. I tried turning them to a different angle. Tried to see if maybe the sunlight was hitting them the wrong way. Perhaps...

Nope.

Leroy. Fucking some white dude.

My Leroy.

As in my boyfriend. As in the man I planned to marry. As in the guy whose apartment I lived in.

I tried angling the photograph again.

Nope.

Whoever took these photos was incredibly talented. These weren't from just some camera on a phone.

Nope.

Telephoto lens from...

I closed my eyes and tried to picture our ground-floor apartment. With the privacy fence... My eyes popped open.

Yep.

The guy who took these—although admittedly it might've been a woman—had to have climbed the tree in the park behind our apartment complex.

This was all kinds of sleazy. And definitely illegal. Big-time illegal.

Yet, I didn't blame the photographer. Well, perhaps a bit. I kind of liked living in ignorance. I could no longer live in denial. The proof sat in my hands as I got fingerprints on the beautiful glossy shots.

"Noah?" Christian sauntered up the walkway to his house.

I sat on the front stoop. Moping.

He offered the boyish grin I expected. My best friend was the happiest guy I knew. Despite all the shit that'd happened to him.

"What's wrong?" His voice took on urgency since I didn't respond to him right away.

Emotion clogged my throat. I held the photographs out to him.

He tossed his messenger bag next to me, then snagged the photographs. Slowly, he flipped through them—one by one.

I knew. What he saw. What he thought.

How stupid I was.

Because, frankly, how could he not? He had proof of Leroy's cheating in his hands. He had proof of my idiocy before him.

Don't ever call yourself an idiot. Christian's words circled in my mind. He was so adamant that I never be hard on myself. I always believed him fanciful and, in this moment, I didn't believe I was worthy of...self-worth. Clearly, I was an idiot.

Slowly, he held his hand out.

I gave him the envelope the photos came in. Just my name in block script with a black pen. Absolutely nothing remarkable about anything. Nothing to give me a hint as to the sender—either their identity or their motive.

Christan tucked the photographs back into the envelope.

I had a vague thought of fingerprints, but quickly dismissed that thought. No way was I taking this to the police. I should be thanking the anonymous photographer—not giving the police the evidence to arrest the man, or woman, who had lifted the veil from my eyes.

Who had destroyed my happiness.

Whatever. Move on.

My best friend tucked the envelope into his messenger bag and plopped next to me on the stoop. "I won't ask you if you're okay, because clearly, you're not. Nor should you be. That sucks."

"That *fucking* sucks."

He chuckled. "Yeah, that too." He didn't swear, so he didn't repeat my words. He slung an arm over my shoulder and pulled me close.

I went willingly—reveling in his strength. He only had a couple of inches on me, but he was a big, broad guy. If he had more padding and less muscle, he could pass for a teddy bear. He definitely had the temperament for one. Unlike me, who could be...sharp. I was muscular and slender. That made me more angles and fewer curves.

"What are you going to do?" He rubbed my shoulder.

"I should confront him, right? And then I should dump his ass, right? And then..." I floundered. Then I sighed, which turned into a sob. "I live in his apartment, for fuck's sake. So, either I move back in with Mom—and the charmer who's there now—or I try to find a place of my own. In this town?" My voice broke on that as well.

The factory, the main employer in town, had recently gone on a hiring spree. People from all over the state—and even beyond—came for the jobs. Not great jobs, but—given the economy—any job was appreciated. The newcomers had snapped up every rental and cheap house in town.

Mom worked for the factory, and she had a nice, two-bedroom apartment. Which was great when we were just the two of us. But became super crowded when one of her skeezy boyfriends was living with us. More frequently, of late—which was why I'd moved in with Leroy. "Why, Christian? Why did he cheat? Why was I not enough? Why am I never enough?" For my dad, who took off. For my mom, who is always looking for the next *one* to fill up the empty well inside her soul. For, apparently, Leroy.

"That's above my paygrade." Christian tipped my chin up so our gazes met. "Only you can figure out stuff like that, Noah. Or you can see a therapist to work through your issues."

I thought he was kidding, but seriousness radiated from those soft-green eyes.

He smiled. A little wistful. A little melancholy. All empathy. "Look, if you could do anything, go anywhere, what would you do?"

I blinked. The answer sure as shit wasn't to move back in with my mother and live in this factory town for the rest of my life. I worked as a teller in the bank, but I was still tied to the factory's fortunes—whether I liked it or not. I took a deep breath. "I'd move to Foggy Basin in California and start a dog-training business."

"Why Foggy Basin?"

"Because I read this tourist brochure and it sounds amazing. Small town, friendly, and in Northern California. Nice climate. I guess..." I hesitated. What was I trying to say? "Fresh start, you know? On the other side of the country."

Christian smiled. "Then let's do it."

"What?"

"Let's do it. We can pack up and go. Do you have to give two weeks' notice at the bank?"

"They owe me two weeks' vacation. I could just take it and not come back." Again, I blinked. "We? You'd come with me?"

"Yes, us together. Absolutely. Get away from this place. I'm not needed here. Every time the Frankstons see me, they're embarrassed. And Laura can't come home and hold her head high because I'm still here. If I go, then she can come home."

Laura was Christian's ex-fiancée. The woman who'd broken his heart. Yet, in this moment, he only thought of her and her comfort with being able to show her face in town after what she'd done to him.

Personally, I was tempted to put the photos of Leroy cheating on me all over the internet. Hell, the town square as well. Except I didn't want pity and, to my surprise, I didn't recognize the other dude who was getting ass fucked by my soon-to-be ex. I could accidentally ruin some rando's life. That wasn't me. Taking down a creepoid ex? Sure. Destroying someone I didn't know? Wasn't in me. "Together?"

"Yep. You and me. I'll get a retail job, and you can do your dog stuff. We'll split the bills." He offered the grin women often swooned over.

I'd thought Laura was one of Christian's admirers. Clearly, I'd been wrong.

"Just like that?" This felt way too easy.

"Dad's going to blow a gasket if I tell him I'm quitting, so I vote we just pack our cars and go."

For the umpteenth time, I blinked. "We can't just pick up and drive across..." I squinted, bringing a map of the States in my mind. "Six? Seven states?"

"Seven," he confirmed. "If we go that way."

How he knew which way I was thinking of was beyond me, but the number of states so was *not* the issue. "It's thirty-one hours of driving."

"So we'll stop a couple of times. We'll drive together. I'll listen to a bunch of audiobooks, and you'll mainline country music." He mock-winced.

An ongoing joke between us. We lived in Tennessee, and only one of us liked country music.

The Black dude.

"You know which album I'm listening to." Somehow, this was becoming real.

"Lovely album, fantastic singer, great pipes, superb humanitarian, and I still would rather listen to Greek for 30 hours."

"Greek?"

He grinned. "You know the expression, *it's all Greek to me*? That's what country music is to me."

I sighed. "You're missing out on a cultural phenomenon."

"As you tell me often. I suspect you'll be playing her album often in our new home?" He offered a baleful expression with his mouth drooping.

Our home. For reasons I didn't understand, that didn't feel monumental. Christian was just pointing out we'd find a place to live together. I'd listen to my country music, he'd play his classical—Bach being a favorite—and we'd coexist in a small space. Possibly a place smaller than the one-bedroom I was sharing with my asshat ex. "Leroy is in Jackson visiting his mother."

Christian gave me *that* look.

Fuck.

I winced. "I honestly thought he was."

"Maybe he is. That's not to say he's not getting some ass on the side." He gestured to his messenger bag—the one with all the photos inside it.

"He's cheating on me."

"That's entirely possible."

"So, I should pack and we should go first thing in the morning."

"That's advisable. I can pack what I need in my room. Mom's got Ladies' Tea and Dad's got work. I can load the car, and we can be on the road by ten."

"Just like that?" This felt way too monumental to be doing anything so rash.

He checked his watch. "If you drive straight to the bank and tender your resignation, and take the accrued vacation, then yeah, that simple. Didn't you say Lettie's daughter wanted a job at the bank?"

"Yeah. Kitty." Because, of course, our town's biggest gossip would name her daughter with the same double consonant as herself.

"Give Kitty a recommendation. Even if she's a total bomb, you'll be long gone."

"Kitty's actually pretty smart."

"Great! So you're helping her out and giving the bank no reason to complain. You might not need a recommendation to get a new job—especially if you're running your own business—but I say you should never burn bridges."

"If we go, I'm never coming back."

"Neither am I."

"But Christian..." I floundered. "Your family, your friends, your job...they're all here."

"I could say the same for you. And yet, we're off on an adventure. Call me tonight when you're packing? We can decide what we can take, what we can donate, and what we can throw out."

"Can I *accidentally* donate Leroy's beloved baseball card collection?"

Christian arched an eyebrow. "I don't see why not. He keeps it with his sex toys, right?"

"I cannot believe I told you that." Whether I meant about the sex toys, the baseball card collection, or the fact they shared a drawer, I wasn't certain.

He sighed dramatically. "These are the things we must bear. Charity shop opens at ten—it'll be our last stop on the way out of town. If Leroy moves fast enough, he might be able to rescue the collection before they sell it. Regardless, I'd say you're good."

We both knew I wasn't...but I honestly didn't care. I'd staked my future on Leroy—and he'd gone and cheated on me. In our bed. Sleazy didn't begin to cover it. And anyway, he didn't have any particularly valuable cards—he just liked to boast he *had a collection*. A claim about as vacuous as he was. "Let's do this." I patted Christian's thigh. "You're a good friend."

"Your best friend," he reminded me.

"Yeah, that." We'd been besties since the first day of first grade.

Some third-grade bully had been trying to steal Christian's expensive sneakers.

I'd fought the kid off and had earned a bloody nose for my trouble. To this day, I kept thinking *how did that kid think he'd get away with stealing sneakers and no one would notice*? Even hearing this was something he did often didn't square. Defied logic.

That said, no one ever tried to pick on Christian again. Being the only son of one of the factory owners made him different.

His parents, and their business partners, controlled much of what happened in town. Fortunes were made and destroyed based on who was favored. Losing one's job could destroy a family. Getting a promotion could lead to prosperity.

And yet Christian was walking away from his inheritance. Frankston and Carter was an institution in our town. Christian was the Carter legacy.

"Okay, I'll drive to the bank right now and tender my resignation."

"Make sure they give you the full vacation you're entitled to. It would be unfortunate if I were to withdraw all my money this afternoon." He winked.

"We'll need to find a bank in California. Or a credit union. Once we have a place to live. Oh shit, what if—"

He pressed a finger to my lips. "While you're finding creative ways to make Leroy pay for his betrayal, I'll search for rentals in Foggy Basin. We'll have something lined up before we cross the state line."

I didn't ask whether he meant Tennessee or California, because it didn't matter. If Christian said something was going to happen, then it did. Simple as that. "Okay."

He patted my shoulder. "Go forth and get it done."

"Yeah."

Just over twelve hours later, we pulled out of our town and headed toward a new beginning.

Chapter One

Christian

"This is so quaint." I grinned as I examined the two-story white house with gingerbread accents. Well, the cut-wood trim probably had a more official name but, to me, the house looked like a gingerbread house would—only white instead of light brown.

Noah leaned against my SUV next to me as we surveyed our new home. We'd driven through the heart of Foggy Basin to get here—which had only been a few square blocks. This town was tiny. So much smaller than the town we'd come from.

This house stood on several acres of fenced, flat grassland. Perfect for running a dog-training center. Our landlady, a charming woman named Miss Esmeralda, had lived here her entire life, but recently had fallen, broken her hip, and been forced to move into a nursing home. She knew she was likely never coming back to her childhood home, but she also couldn't bear to part with it. She had enough in her inheritance to cover her nursing-care home costs, but a little rental income would help ease things. More importantly, she wanted to know her home was well-cared-for.

Two enterprising young men, one of whom was starting a business, were just the sort of tenants she was looking for.

Personally, I'd question two single dudes from out of state with no references, but something about me reassured her. Or so she'd claimed during our three-hour marathon conversation while I'd been hunkered down in a cheap motel in Texas. I'd tried not to let desperation leach into my voice. Just...I promised Noah I'd take care of this. That everything would be perfect.

So it just had to be.

Because I was sort of in love with Noah and wanted the best for him.

Sort of? Sheesh, who are you trying to deceive?

Yeah, no two ways about it. I was head over heels in love with Noah Gainey.

"It's better than I expected." Noah tilted his head the way he always did when he was deep in thought.

"Miss Esmeralda did warn me it's *old-lady furniture and decorating,* but that we could put the excess furniture and knickknacks in the attic or cellar." I sighed. "She knows she's not coming back, and she's still trying to figure out who will deal with her estate when she passes, but she's got a few years left." *Or so she maintained.* Once we were settled, I would fulfill my promise to her and go visit properly. We'd picked up the keys at the sheriff's office where the man himself had given us a bit of a grilling.

Sheriff Clayton West was about forty, with brown hair and piercing blue eyes that saw everything and missed nothing. He gave us the lay of the land and made it clear we were expected to be law-abiding citizens, and respectful of all—especially Miss Esmeralda.

We didn't mind the third degree. We had nothing to hide.

I held the keys out to Noah.

After a long moment, he took them. "This feels too good to be true. How do we know there aren't bodies stacked inside? That the place isn't coated in blood? Maybe human heads in formaldehyde jars in the basement?"

"You sure can be morbid." I grinned. "The sheriff locked up the place after Miss Esmeralda went to the hospital. After having met the guy, I can confidently say he did an inventory of everything. And I mean *everything*. If so much as a doily goes missing, he'll track us down."

A laugh burst from Noah's chest. "Okay." He clutched the keys. "Doilies go in a box to the attic. I've hated your mother's doilies since I accidentally spilled chocolate sauce on one when I was eight." He pursed his lips.

Drat. I'd forgotten about that incident. Shouldn't have mentioned doilies. I wracked my mind for any other potential triggers. The truth was, Noah was a sensitive soul, and when someone hurt him—whether intentionally or not—he felt that hurt down to the marrow of his bones.

Hence the reason Leroy's cheating had been such a blow to my good friend.

Sunny days from here on out.

Noah pushed off my SUV and headed up the walkway to the house. He opened the gate, then held it for me. After I stepped through, he closed it. "We need to get into the habit of always closing it. I plan to go along the fence line carefully to ensure it's intact."

"Of course." I wasn't going to point out the thing had only been installed five years ago. Miss Esmeralda had grown tired of rabbits eating her lettuce and carrots. Only some seriously determined dogs would be able to jump the fence.

We mounted the steps.

"I love this veranda." I pointed to the swing for two. "I can't wait to just sit and watch the sunset."

Noah squinted as he pivoted to look out. "How do you know which direction everything is?"

"Google maps."

"Ah." He might've spent the last five years working on a computer as a bank teller, but he sure didn't enjoy them otherwise.

I was always prodigiously careful not to point out that his phone was just a minicomputer. That wouldn't have gone over very well.

He unlocked the door and gestured for me to go first.

Ever the gentleman. He didn't always come across that way—especially with his potty mouth and cynical attitude—but he rescued kittens from trees, helped aging ladies across the street, and always gave due deference to his elders.

Well, most of his elders. He had no time for my parents and their shenanigans.

And I didn't blame him.

The front hall was a little dark, so I hit the light switch.

The sheriff explained how he'd shuttered the place as best he could, so all the blinds were closed, the air conditioning had been turned off, and all the perishables removed from the fridge.

For which I was incredibly grateful. "Shall we open the drapes? Miss Esmeralda's only been gone a couple of weeks. She used to have a cleaner come in once a month. Nice young fellow whom she highly recommends—"

"We can probably manage our own cleaning." Noah gave me a once-over. "Well, I can. Do you even know how to hold a duster?"

"I'm assuming I hold the handle in my hand?" I raised my arm and purposely made my wrist limp.

He nudged me. "God, you're an asshole."

A comment at which I took precisely zero offense. He loved assholes. Well, except when he didn't. Tone of voice usually gave me the direction I needed to know where he was headed with a thought. "I'm capable of cleaning." I hadn't...but that didn't mean I couldn't learn. "Although I will be occupied finding employment." I stalked into the parlor and threw the drapes open.

Huh. Not as much dust as I expected.

"What employment are you planning to seek?" Noah followed me in. "You've been a junior executive in your family's company since finishing business school. I don't know how many executive jobs there are in Foggy Basin." He eyed me dubiously, with a little furrow between his brows.

"I'll cope." I grinned. "I always land on my feet."

The furrow deepened.

"What?" I stepped closer to the very floral pink- and-white sofa. And eyed the side table with its shocking amount of lace in the cloth.

"You've never had to struggle, Christian." He rubbed his face. "Which is why I don't understand why you're doing it now. I mean, how much money were you able to bring with you?"

I squinted as if I was doing some quick math in my head. "Enough for a few weeks." I crossed my fingers at the blatant lie. "I'll need to find employment straight away, but I don't believe that will be difficult. This town has a robust service-and-goods sector."

"A what?"

"I plan to get a job in a store."

He blinked. "Doing what? You think they'll just make you a manager?"

"Of course not. I intend to work as an employee. Cashier, or greeter, or sales assistant." I tilted my head as I examined a table lamp, trying to find the switch. Oh, as part of the cord. Well, why not? "Why don't we check out the dining room before proceeding into the kitchen?"

"You're as formal as this house." Noah nudged me. "Yeah, we can do that."

He'd been teasing me for twenty years about my formality. Still, my parents had ingrained in me that Carters behaved a certain way. That much was expected of them. And I'd done everything I could to meet those expectations. Even going so far as to remain at home until I married—so as to not be living a profligate life.

Well, you can see how well that went.

My parents had, collectively, left about twenty-two messages on my phone.

I need to get a new number. The few acquaintances whom I trusted to not share that new number would receive a text before I shuttered the Tennessee number entirely.

Noah's phone had, to the best of what I could see, been silent.

Hope he blocked Leroy.

My friend didn't need that riffraff in his life.

The formal dining room stunned with its elegance and a table that sat twenty.

Noah caught my gaze and arched an eyebrow.

I grinned. "We're going to have so many friends that they won't all fit at the table."

He snorted.

Of the two of us, I'd always had more faith in positivity. Which, given my family's predicament, I really wasn't entitled to. "I believe this room will require much dusting." I moved to the china cabinet that bore a stunning blue-and-white Delft pattern on display. "I don't recall Miss Esmeralda mentioning she had Dutch heritage. Somehow..." I considered. "I figured she would have..."

"Floral?" Noah pointed to the large canvas of a vase overflowing with pink roses.

"She painted that." I grinned. "She's an accomplished painter and, to the best of her memory, she has at least six of her paintings displayed. Another eight or ten are in the attic. She likes to rotate them. Oh, we must find those and honor the tradition." Excitement grew within me.

"Are they all—" Noah tilted his head. "Pink?"

"I didn't ask. She volunteered the history of the artwork and, after some cajoling on my behalf, imparted the news of her talent. I promised to take photographs of all the works and have them framed in a collage for her to keep at the nursing home. I offered to bring them to her in a rotation, but she felt her work was too dignified for that." I leaned in closer, as if sharing some great secret. "I believe she's embarrassed for people to know her talent."

"Exactly how long were you talking to her?"

"Three hours."

He blinked. "When was this?"

"The night you watched the Titans game. Well, you attempted to watch the game. You were quite fatigued, and when I returned to our room, you were fast asleep."

With great care, I'd covered him with a blanket—then I'd lain awake on my bed and just watched him for more than an hour. Longing had gripped me, as it so often did. I'd never tell him, of course, how I felt. Plus, he always broke up with his boyfriends, and I didn't want to lose our friendship.

Or so you tell yourself. Secretly, you wish he'd pick you, and that you'd settle down, marry, raise dogs, and be together forever.

All that was true. But I lived in the real world—not the world of fairy tales.

"I believe the kitchen is this way." I gestured toward the back of the house.

Noah went first, pushing swinging doors into a cavernous room which contained both the family room and the kitchen.

I examined the floor. "Oh, these used to be two different rooms with a wall between them. I wondered at this very modern design of one large space." I did some mental calculations. "The kitchen would have been quite cramped." I pointed. "They removed the wall and added this center island. Quite clever."

"Hopefully they didn't remove a retaining wall." Noah pointed to the television. "Okay, that's got to go."

I squinted. "Is it even color? I believe that is a cathode-ray-tube television."

"Fucking hell." He slashed the air.

"What?"

"I should've stolen Leroy's television. Ninety-eight-inch, ultra-high-def, 4k..." He rubbed his hands against his face.

"I believe the key word in that sentence was *stolen*. You already liberated him of his treasured baseball card collection—"

"Nothing of value in there."

"Isn't value in the eye of the beholder?"

He lowered his hand from his face. "That's beauty."

"Well, he didn't behold that either." I sniffed. "Still, stealing is beneath you. We shall purchase a new television. I didn't see an electronics store in town, but surely there must be a larger location where we can pick up a few things."

"We can't just blow several thousand dollars on a television." He approached the tiny one on the overly large stand. "I can't even plug in my gaming system."

That he hadn't stolen. He'd simply, since it was his, added it to his rather pathetic stash of belongings. He wasn't an accumulator or collector of things. No, his gift was with interpersonal relationships.

Or so I told myself.

"Look, I have a laptop. Sheriff West said the internet is still connected. Miss Esmeralda had little time for television, but she loved reading books on her tablet." The sheriff had nicely collected that for her along with a few other essentials.

I'd asked if she needed anything else, and she replied that once I visited her in the nursing home and she *got my measure* that she'd decide. For my part, I anticipated with great joy meeting this...quirky...lady. "We can connect my laptop and order whatever we need. Surely there's a company that delivers this far. We aren't a million miles from civilization."

"Given the circumference of the earth is just forty-thousand miles? Yes, no one is a million miles from civilization." Noah ran his finger along the top of the television. "I had other plans for your laptop."

I blinked. "You're not watching porn on my—"

He burst out laughing. "Uh, no." He closed his left eye. "I can do that on my phone."

"Oh."

"I was hoping..." He twisted his fingers together.

"Yes...?"

"That you might help me design a website. I need to start finding clients right away. I mean, might as well put all those training classes to use."

When Noah hadn't been working as a bank teller, or sleeping with the wrong men, he'd been an assistant trainer at a pet store. He'd been in line for a promotion to head trainer—and an ability to quit his day job and live his dream—when Leroy the scumbag had cheated.

"I will be most pleased to assist you in setting up your website. Let's unpack our vehicles, shower, eat dinner at that lovely diner we saw, and then come back to commence work. By bedtime, we'll have the best website possible. You have custody of the photographs?"

"Yep. Thanks for reminding me to do that."

The pet store had a large collection of photographs of Noah with the different pets he'd trained. I'd advised him to get digital copies along with a legal release so he could use them for his own purposes. The trainer he worked with adored him and so had cajoled the store owners into providing everything we needed. Since Noah wasn't competing for business, they were also willing to provide references.

Several of Noah's clients had provided testimonials.

I had everything I needed. The mandatory marketing class I'd attended, along with the elective on website design, would come in handy. "All good."

His eyes softened. "What would I do without you?"

"You need never find out. I'll always have your back."

"As I'll always have yours." He said the words reflexively—likely with little thought to them. We'd been sharing them back and forth for nearly twenty years.

But I wanted so very much more.

"Does this place meet your standards? Are you ready to unpack?"

He grinned. "I can't wait to start our new lives."

Oh, I really hope so.

Chapter Two

Noah

The Blue Star Diner was classic Americana—and I loved it.

Andrew, an adorable guy with golden-brown hair and the co-owner, greeted us with a huge smile. "New in town or passing through?"

I met his grin. "New in town. We've rented a house just outside of town."

"Oh, whose house? If you don't mind me asking. I know just about everyone around here."

"Miss Esmeralda's home." Christian added his smile to our little group as Andrew guided us to a booth.

"I was so sad to hear she went into the nursing home—but for the best, I think. She was so very independent." The young man gestured for us to slide in.

"We're going to visit her once she's settled and she invites us." I eased into the booth with vinyl seats. "And I'm starting to ramp up my business."

After he placed the menus on the table, Andrew cocked his hip. "Business?"

"Dog training."

"Oh! I love it. There are a couple of people in town who can definitely use your services. Whether they will or not is an entirely different story. Do you have a business card?"

"I do." I yanked out my wallet and handed over three cards. We'd had these printed at a store in Sacramento as we passed through so we'd be ready to go when we arrived. "I have flyers as well."

"The library. Maybe the feed store? They're just out of town. And I'd suggest the rec center in Hartsville. There's a pet store as well."

"Hartsville?"

"Yeah, oh, and maybe the hardware store? The owner's a friendly guy..." Andrew grinned.

"May I ask a question?"

He pivoted his attention to me now, watching me with intensely curious eyes. "Sure."

"I'm looking for a job. Now, I'm a hard worker."

"That's a given," Noah muttered.

I shot him a look.

He held up his hands.

"What kind of job are you looking for? Depending on the time of year—hell, depending on the year—work can be scarce or it can be abundant. These days? Try Dillon over at the grocery store. I think he's looking for someone to stock shelves. It's not glamorous—"

"It's perfect." I grinned goofily. "That's exactly what I'm looking for."

"Well, okay, then. Foggy Basin Grocers. You really can't miss it. Dillon's...well, you'll see." He offered a sweet smile as he tucked my cards into his pocket. "Gabriella will be here to help you shortly. Welcome to town." He sauntered off and, as we watched, a handsome, tanned-skin police officer, in uniform, walked into the diner.

Andrew stepped right into his embrace, and they kissed.

I chanced a glance at Christian. As I watched, his frown morphed into a sappy smile. "I think I'm going to like this town."

"Hey, I thought you already did. You were certainly gung-ho when I proposed it."

"I didn't know much about it. I will say my conversations with Esmeralda definitely swayed me." He offered me a smile. "Anywhere you are is home to me." He bit his lower lip. "That came out wrong."

"Nothing wrong about it. You're home to me as well. Just no longer in Tennessee. Here? Nestled in the tranquility of Northern California with national forests on both sides? Temperate climate? Decent-size city within a couple hours' drive? We're in nature, Christian. Can't you just smell the fresh air?"

He inhaled. "French fries, frying meat, ketchup and... Huh. Something...but I wasn't certain what." He cocked his head. "I will admit this is exciting. As far away from Tennessee as we can pretty much get."

"Unless we went to Alaska or Hawaii." My grin never faltered.

"As you said, temperate climate." He straightened his cutlery on his napkin. He had a habit of doing that and probably didn't even realize it.

"Well, California could get hot like Hawaii, but never as cold as Alaskan winters. Nope, this town is just right. Kind of like Goldilocks when she found the right bed."

"What can I get you today?" A young woman with black hair and dark-brown eyes offered a warm smile.

"Gabriella?" I returned her grin.

"Yes." She gazed back and forth between the two of us. "New in town?"

"Yep." I continued to grin like a loon.

"Well, watch out for the cops. They're big on giving speeding tickets. My brother's one of them, and you don't want to upset him."

For a moment, I wondered about her warning.

Then she added, "But he's married to Andrew, my boss—so no stealing him."

"We saw them together earlier. They make a cute couple."

She grinned.

Then, I had a moment to ponder, but Christian beat me to it. "We're not *together* together. We're best friends."

"Oh. My mistake." Although she didn't appear the least bit chagrinned. "I see so many gay people hooking up that maybe I see couples where they don't exist."

Why would she think Christian and I were together? Although maybe she somehow senses I'm gay? The rainbow bracelet might give her that idea...

"What would you like?"

"I'll have the chicken fingers and fries." I always chose unhealthy when we came to a place like this. Given I ate healthy most of the rest of the time, this felt fair to me.

"I'll have a burger and a salad, thank you." Christian handed Gabriella the menus.

"Could I get extra fries?" I eyed him. "He always steals some of mine."

"Hey."

I arched an eyebrow.

He crossed his arms. Then, after a moment, relented. "I might resemble that comment."

Gabriella laughed. "Oh, I think I like you." She winked and headed back in the direction of the kitchen.

"Well, that took you thirty seconds." I toyed with my napkin.

He blinked. "What *took thirty seconds?*"

"You finding someone to flirt with. You should ask her out. She's a little young, though." Although we were probably only a few years older than her. Still, she was damn attractive. Although the older cop brother might be an issue.

"I wasn't flirting. She had a vibrant personality—" He gesticulated in a way I didn't understand.

"She's gorgeous."

He pursed his lips. "I don't select potential future partners based on their looks." Even as he said the words, though, he sort of petered off. His eyes took on a dreamy quality that I noticed every once in a while.

Must be thinking about Laura again. Damn shame she had to run off and leave him high and dry. They would've made a stunning couple. Except if they'd married, then I might be in Foggy Basin alone. That idea made me sad. "Christian."

He blinked. "Sorry."

I waved my hand as if to indicate I hadn't meant anything by calling him. Except I had. I wanted details he'd never shared with me.

He snagged my hand. "Please say whatever you were going to say."

"Uh—" I held his gaze, then looked down where he held my hand. Warm fuzzies enveloped me, as they always did. Touching Christian always grounded me in a way few other things did.

"Right." He released me. "Wouldn't want to give people the wrong impression."

"Gabriella in particular."

He sighed. "Even if she's single—which she might not be—"

"She was flirting with you—"

"—Even if she's single," he repeated. "I'm not interested."

"You're not over Laura. You need to meet someone new. Have...new experiences."

"I don't need new experiences." He held my gaze. "I'm fine just the way I am."

"I didn't mean—"

"But you did." He cut me off. "Everyone always assumes that to be happy with one's life, one must be in a relationship. That precludes the notion that someone can be alone and happy. Take Miss Esmeralda. She's alone, and yet has assured me she's very happy. Being in a relationship doesn't always alleviate loneliness. My parents have been married for thirty years, yet I wouldn't say either is happy. Or not lonely. It's all by degrees. I have you in my life as a best friend. Ergo, I am not alone."

"But you're not—" I gazed around to ensure we were alone. "—getting laid."

"One does not have to have sex to be happy. Asexual people can be very happy without the benefit of regular..." He rolled his hand.

"Penetrative sex?"

"One order of chicken fingers with extra fries and one burger with a side salad. I forgot to ask your preference in dressing and if you want gravy." Gabriella gazed back and forth between Christian and me.

I was quite certain I'd be scarlet, if not for my skin tone. Undoubtedly, she'd heard the *penetrative sex* comment. I wasn't a prude—far from it. But I didn't generally have conversations like this. And never in public. Also, clearly never with Christian because I had no idea about the asexual thing. *He didn't actually say he was asexual—just that asexual people were fine without sex. And even some people who aren't asexual are happy without sex. And, for the record, I've had lots of sex and I'm not all that happy.* Well, unless I was with Christian.

"Uh, ranch is great." He ducked his head.

"I'll take some gravy." I kept my voice strong—as if I wasn't humiliated by using such graphic language in public.

"Be right back." Gabriella hustled away.

"Christian?"

"Uh-huh."

"Look at me?"

Clearly, he wanted to say *no*, because he almost never said no to me. That wasn't his nature. Actually, I knew he had a difficult time saying *no* to anyone. Which might've been how he wound up here with me—in Foggy Basin. "We're going to find you someone, okay?"

Finally, he met my gaze. "I don't want to meet someone. I'm fine."

I snagged a fry and waved it at him as an idea coalesced in my mind. "Operation Find Christian a Girlfriend begins today."

He groaned.

Probably he thought I couldn't hear—but I could. I had excellent hearing.

"Noah—"

"No. It's time you put Laura in the rearview mirror and move on with your life. I know you were humiliated—"

"Gee, thanks."

"—but I think it's important that you find someone you can spend your life with."

"Like you?"

That fry, midway to my mouth, dropped to the plate.

"I'm done with me, okay? Fresh start means no more dating assholes." *Shit.* I glanced around. No Gabriella— Okay, she was making her way to us.

"One bowl of gravy and some ranch dressing. Anything else?"

"This is perfect." My chicken fingers had come with a side of plum sauce, so I was literally in heaven.

"Okay." She pointed to our plates. "Too hot?"

Crap. We hadn't taken a bite. "Uh, an intense conversation. Just trying to figure out who's single in this town?"

"Oh, lots of people." She toyed with her apron. "I've got a friend, Joanie. She's super cute and has a great sense of humor. I can call her—"

"No." Christian said the words quickly. "But that's awfully nice of you. I'm not actually looking."

Gabriella pivoted her attention to me.

"Very gay and very not looking."

She furrowed her brow as if trying to piece together why I'd just asked how to figure out who was single while simultaneously not looking for, uh, single people.

"If either of you change your mind, I know several single women." She gave Christian *that* look. "I also know some gay single guys, and I know my brother could put out feelers—" Her gaze fell to me.

"Really appreciative. I've just...sworn off men for a while."

"Oh, I get that. I could tell you about—"

"Gabriella? The order's up." Andrew's voice rang out.

"Oops. We're super busy. Later." With a little wave, she hustled back to the kitchen.

Christian cut his burger in half—as was his custom—and gave me one long look. "Watch out for turnabout. All's fair in love and war."

In other words—don't rock the boat. I'm happy with things the way they are now.

I saluted him with a fry.

While totally trying to figure out how I was going to find a guy.

Chapter Three

Christian

The grocery store on Main Street felt a bit different from the ones in the big cities I'd visited. Small-town stores always had a feeling about them—like a new friend might be around the corner of each aisle.

Dillon McKay was cute in a boy-next-door kind of way. His eyes assessed me as I explained the reason for my visit. "So, Andrew at the Blue Star Diner mentioned you might be hiring."

"A stock-person position. Well, I'd say *stock boy*, but that's not inclusive because I'd hire a competent woman just as much as I'd hire a guy. But you?" He scratched his chin. "Your résumé doesn't exactly scream *I'm good at stocking shelves.*"

I considered his words. "I'm excellent at completing tasks in a rapid manner. I'm good at taking directions and following them precisely. I'm a hard worker, and I'll never let you down."

"Those are, uh, big promises." He eyed me with those penetrating gray-colored eyes that went adorably with his ash-blond hair. Like he was trying to see my sincerity. To test my veracity. To determine if I was good to my word. "And you can't provide references?"

"That's tough." I wrinkled my nose. "I left the family firm in...a bit of a hurry. Not that I'd ever do that to you," I rushed to add. "Just my friend Noah decided he needed a fresh start, and he chose Foggy Basin. I decided instead of being a corporate lackey for the rest of my life that I'd follow him. The family firm will remain standing whether I'm there or not." *At least I hope it will. Bit of challenge with my family's finances, but that's not my problem.* I offered up what Noah always called my *winning* smile.

"Sure, we can give this a try. It's a physically demanding job."

"I've never backed down from something that might be hard. I just need a job."

Dillon held out his hand.

I put my hand in his. *Strong grip. But not overpowering.* The guy was objectively attractive, but I didn't feel any spark. Nope, that gnawing feeling of need was only ever for Noah.

Thirty minutes later, after having completed all the necessary paperwork, I had a job with a nametag and an apron. Also, I had a schedule for the next week—working Tuesday to Saturday. Kind of sucked that I'd be working for part of the weekend, but Noah might not be working regular hours anyway.

I'd barely stepped outside when Noah pounced.

Metaphorically—not literally.

"You'll never guess what happened."

I put my sunglasses on and considered wandering toward the car, but my friend's enthusiasm clearly couldn't be contained. "Honestly, Noah, I wouldn't even know where to begin guessing."

"Well, I drove to the feed store—just outside of town. They sell dog food." He gestured to the grocery store. "Way more than their collection."

"Okay. Well, I'm going to assume you weren't buying dog food for us."

"Duh, no." His dark-brown eyes sparkled.

"Tell me." Truthfully, when he was this happy, I was content to just let him bask in whatever had brought on this euphoria. Because life always came crashing down on him. Just an inevitability that I hated for him. Just once—just one single time—I wished nothing bad would happen to him. That his happiness just went on and on and on. But that wasn't how life worked. Usually, for him, things crashed when he started dating some loser who eventually broke his heart.

"I met a lady with a puppy." He vibrated with excitement.

"Okay." The trajectory of this conversation was becoming clear.

"And she was complaining she couldn't find a trainer in town."

"And of course you offered her a business card."

"Yep." A grin split his face. "Labrador puppy."

"That sounds great. Will she be coming—"

"And she's in a group chat with the owners of the other ten puppies from the litter."

I did some quick—and very simple—math in my head. "Eleven puppies?"

"Yep." He grinned. "And the owners are from as far as Sacramento, Miller's Point, and Hartsville—but they're all looking for a good trainer. Somehow, in five minutes, she got eight of them to agree to come out to our place on Sunday afternoons at noon for group lessons starting next weekend."

Again, I did the math in my head. Nine puppies times a minimum of eight weeks and— "Oh, wow."

"Yeah!" He grabbed me and pulled me into a hug.

I went willingly.

"That will cover all of my startup expenses with some money left for household expenses. This is huge."

He wasn't kidding.

"And I explained how I did puppy, beginner, advanced, tricks, and therapy-dog classes. Glynnis said she wanted all five. She visits a nursing home in Hartsville, and the therapy dog who used to visit retired." He let me go suddenly—as if suddenly realizing he still held me.

I felt bereft, but kept that feeling to myself. "And...?"

"She adopted the puppy with the hopes of eventually training it to be a therapy dog. Now, Bear's got some attitude—"

"Bear?"

"Right? Anyway, he's already headstrong, and he's only thirteen weeks. I've got my work cut out for me."

"Yeah, no kidding." Noah preferred when people rescued dogs instead of buying puppies from breeders, but he wasn't about to turn down the kind of paid work being presented to him.

"When are they coming? We'll need to make sure we've got the training pen set up."

"A week from Sunday. So, we've got a bit of time." He closed his eyes and blew out a breath of what I knew was frustration. "I didn't even ask how you did." He met my gaze.

I gestured toward where he'd parked "Because your news is far more important. I got the job, and I start Tuesday morning."

"Tuesday?"

"I work Tuesday through Saturday."

"Oh good."

I stopped. "Huh?"

"You'll be around to help with the puppies."

That hadn't occurred to me. He was always so competent, I assumed he could just do everything himself. "Right, of course."

"And there might be one more thing."

Apparently we'd moved off my job, which was just fine. Stocking shelves and occasionally covering the till wasn't all that impressive anyway—even if the job was going to be my first that I didn't get by nepotism. "Yep?"

"We might be going to meet a guy named Paxton."

I squinted. "Am I supposed to know who Paxton is?"

"Nope. But he had a flyer up in the feed store. He found a dog on his property, like, a month ago. He's been trying to find the owner, with no luck. The sheriff confirmed, since Paxton's done his due diligence in trying to find the owner, that he's free to re-home the dog."

I arched an eyebrow. "So, we're taking..."

"Stormy."

"Stormy off of Paxton's hands?"

"He swears she's a really well-behaved dog. He'd love to keep her, but he's got three of his own and a large farm to run. He thinks that might be why she was dumped on his property. The vet, Dr. Malcolm Jones, checked. No microchip or tattoo. He figured she's about nine months old. She likely got bigger than the owners expected, and that's why they dumped her."

"Because why turn a dog over to a shelter and answer all those embarrassing questions when you can just dump a dog in some random farmer's field?"

Noah nodded. "Pretty much."

"Okay. So what do we need to get?"

He cocked his head. "I might've stocked up with everything, and it's in the SUV."

Because of course he did. He'd know I wasn't going to say no. And since I wasn't, his exuberance wasn't an issue. "You have the address for the farmer?"

"Yep. He's expecting us."

"Well let's not keep the gentleman waiting, then."

We resumed our walk.

Suddenly, Noah stopped.

I halted as well, turning to face him. "What's wrong?"

"I didn't ask."

I grinned. "I know you didn't. Because you didn't need to. Of course I was going to say *yes*. I'll always say *yes*." I stepped into his personal space—which I could only get away with because of our long familiarity with each other. "I'll never deny you anything, Noah. Well, within reason. Now come along—we have a dog to rescue."

Chapter Four

Noah

Paxton Greer had a lovely plum farm, and he was happy to give us a tour as Stormy acclimated to us. The Newfie cross was already about eighty pounds and had massive feet.

"The vet reckons she'll be over one hundred." Paxton petted her. "She's a big sweetheart, but I just don't have room for one more."

His three other dogs were penned back near the farmhouse.

He glanced around. "Okay, I'd totally keep her, but my wife would have a conniption fit. She's pregnant with our second child, and she's already got a lot to deal with. I mean, I do what I can, but I'm in the fields a lot."

We wandered down a row of trees in his orchard.

Stormy steadfastly walked on his far side, keeping her distance from Christian and me.

"We'll give her a good home, I promise. We're renting a lovely home on acreage."

"Esmeralda's place?"

I nodded. He'd asked when I'd called, and I'd laid everything on the table. I didn't want to show up, fall in love with Stormy, and then not pass Paxton's inspection. He was trying to play this off like letting Stormy go was no big deal, but it clearly was.

"Noah's a dog trainer." Christian grinned. "He's raised dogs his entire life and is so great with them. Stormy's going to have plenty of company."

"Oh?" Paxton cocked his head.

Christian's eyes widened as if he realized he might've said the wrong thing. He likely hadn't—but I didn't need him championing me. Even if those words made my insides go gooey.

"What he's trying to say is we're starting a class of puppies next week. Stormy's going to show them what a good dog looks like." I eyed her over Paxton's side.

She was an incredibly well-behaved dog. Walking on the leash without pulling. Cautious but not unfriendly with strangers. Attentive and clearly eager to please.

Paxton wiped his brow. "She's had some solid training. I don't understand why someone dumped her here—in the middle of a rainstorm, no less. She came to our door and cowered under the porch. I only saw the flash of her eyes. Thought she might be a coyote or something, but she came right to me. I dried her off, fed her, then spent the next month with a shadow as I've tried to find her owner." He shook his head. "No luck."

"You said you spoke to Sheriff West?"

"Clay. Yeah. He thanked me for watching over her and said I was free to re-home her. I could've gone to a shelter, but I thought maybe I might be able to find someone myself." He eyed me. "Someone who'd see how special she is."

"I can see it. You've done a great job with her. Clearly she's been well treated. I promise we'll take good care of her. Our SUV's full of everything she might need, and we'll run over to Hartsville if there's something she needs that we don't have."

"You can keep the harness. I bought it for her special." Paxton smiled. "And I bought adjustable because she's still growing. I'd say she's putting on almost a pound a week."

"They grow up quickly." I glanced at the dog. "You've been treat training her?"

"Yep. Figured that was the quickest way to gain compliance. The vet said it'd be fine because she's not overweight or anything."

"Great. We bought a bunch, so I'll pick up where you left off." Truthfully, I didn't know how competent Paxton was with training, but Stormy responded well to him. *This is going to hurt her—taking her away from him. From this farm.* Yet she couldn't stay. Christian and I could offer her a good home. "Do you have some paperwork you would like us to sign?"

Paxton nodded. "Nothing legal or anything. Just a document saying you're going to be responsible for her. That you'll get her spayed and micro-chipped. Or tattooed. Doesn't matter. Just that you'll take care of her the way she deserves to be."

"I'm happy to sign any papers. And yes, we'll get her to the vet next week and discuss all those things. I'm a strong believer in…" I hesitated. "They're like my kids. Growing up? I had kind of a chaotic home-life, but I always had an animal to love. Hank, my last rescue, died a year ago. I'd been looking for the next one when I met someone." I cleared my throat. "That didn't pan out, and I missed having an animal in my life. Having a companion. Christian's okay, but he's not so great to cuddle with on the couch."

"Hey!" He tried for indignant, but his grin gave him away.

Paxton gazed between the two of us. "Y'all aren't a couple?"

Christian coughed.

"Oh." I frowned. "I should've been clear. Best friends. We're sharing the house, and although Stormy will be my responsibility, Christian's my backup. Always two of us to take care of her."

The farmer laughed. "You must be close because I totally read you as a couple. Doesn't matter to me. I have a couple of gay friends myself. I'm of the *live and let live* school of thought. Some folks aren't so much." He gestured to my bracelet. "Just don't forget that."

"I won't. I wore it around my town in Tennessee. Including at the bank where I worked. I was always willing to stand up to homophobes."

"Good for you." Paxton petted Stormy on the head. "I don't care about the sexual orientation of whoever she's going to. I just want to know she's cared for."

"We can send regular photo updates, if you'd like. Just quick little check-ins." Christian offered the words with a sincere smile.

"I'd really like that. I'd come visit, but I don't want to confuse her. But yeah, for the first few months, anyway…if you could let me know how she's doing?"

"I have your cell phone number." I eyed Christian even as I spoke to Paxton. "If you don't mind, I'll let him send the updates. It's something he's good at." I was fine with using my phone for business, but I'd never been enamored with it. I preferred face-to-face contact.

Christian lived for messaging and texting. Yet, in time since we'd left home, he hadn't—in my presence—sent a single text.

As a precaution, I'd shut down my one social media account. I'd given my new unlisted number to my mother—who'd appeared wholly uninterested. She was with a new guy and he'd be the center of her universe until he fucked off to wherever.

"Yes." Paxton nodded to Christian. "Thanks for the suggestion."

He smiled back. "I'd want to know, if our positions were reversed."

"Well..." He stopped and gazed around. "You'll have free plums for life. Because you're rescuing her." He smiled—a little wistfully. "All three of mine are rescues. But my wife, rightly, put her foot down at a fourth." He knelt before Stormy. "I adore you so very much. You need to know I would've kept you."

She licked his cheek. She didn't understand the words, of course, but she clearly understood something big was happening and her *person* was upset.

I hated to add to her upheaval, but no easy way existed for us to do this.

Paxton gave her a hug as she leaned against him. Clearly, he'd bonded with her. *This must be killing him. I know it would destroy me.* I'd raised four dogs through my childhood, adolescence, and early adulthood. Losing each had gutted me. I would've loved to say my mother had guided me through the pain, but she hadn't. She'd simply agreed to let me rescue another dog. *As long as they don't get in my way.* Her *way* being whatever guy she was with at the time. I loved my mother, but her taste in men was atrocious.

Paxton rose, handed me the leash, turned, and then walked away.

Stormy tried to follow, but I clicked my tongue. She turned to me.

I pulled a treat out of my pocket.

She cocked her head.

I placed it on the ground between the two of us.

She didn't hesitate, inhaling the treat without even tasting.

"Want another?" I clearly had her attention.

She eyed me.

"Sit."

She plopped onto her butt and eyed the treat. When I offered it on my palm, she lapped it up.

"Good girl. You're such a good girl." I held out my hand.

After a long moment, she placed herself under my hand.

I was able to stroke her long, luscious, silky fur. I'd never had a Newfoundland of my own, but I'd trained one at the store a couple of years ago. Wicked smart and, if raised correctly, incredibly gentle. I trusted that if Paxton had any concerns, he would've voiced them. She'd been living with complete access to three other dogs and a toddler without incident. "Are you ready to come home with us? Oh, you need to meet Christian."

He stepped within her line of sight.

"You can give her a treat."

His eyes lit and he dug into his pocket.

We'd prepared for the visit and the hopeful eventuality that she'd come home with us.

"Treat?" He held it out to her. "Oh, can you go down?"

She plopped onto the dry earth.

"Oh, what a good girl you are. So precious." He was using his cutesy voice that always amused me. I would vary my tone of voice depending on how I was interacting with the dogs—but I never did *cutesy*.

She lapped up the treat he offered.

We were going to be okay.

Chapter Five

Christian

Leaving Stormy in order to go to work nearly broke my heart, but it had to be done.

In turn, I was exhausted when I pulled into the driveway at the end of my first day.

Dillon was a fair employer, a stickler for taking breaks, and a bit anal on how he liked things. That was completely fair—given the store was his. Passed down by his father a little while ago.

He had a growing business, and I was happy to be a part of his team. Stocking proved pretty easy and, with my math skills, running the till wasn't hard. Everything was so fancy these days. Of course, I didn't have many clear memories of the *old days*—what with being Gen Z and all that. I still had nostalgia, however, for a simpler time. Probably the reason I bought paperback books.

In fact, I'd run over to the library during my break to snag a couple. I planned to sit on the veranda, with Stormy at my side and my feet elevated while reading a book and maybe sipping tea.

I'd closed the gate after driving through it, so I wasn't worried about Stormy escaping when she barreled from the house to greet me. "Were you a good girl?"

She plopped onto her butt. Apparently, to her, those words were interpreted as *sit* and *treat*.

I pulled a little treat from my pocket and held it out to her.

Precisely zero hesitation as she lapped it off my hand.

I petted her head, making certain to scratch her ears. "You're the best. Did you have a good day?"

"She did."

Glancing up, I caught sight of Noah lazily walking down the couple of steps from the house and then sauntering over to us. He looked positively yummy in a tight T-shirt and jeans that hugged his frame. "Glad to hear it."

He stopped about a foot away from me. "How'd you manage?"

"First time I ever did manual labor." I grinned. "I loved it. Am exhausted and want a shower, but...yeah, feeling really good."

"Why don't you soak in the tub? I made a grilled chicken salad for tonight. The day's been warm, and I didn't want anything heavy." He eyed me. "Obviously you've just burned a ton of calories and need a real—"

"Chicken salad is a real meal, and it's one of my favorites. Thank you." I had the absurd desire to kiss him as thanks, but that would've been just weird.

Right?

Right. "Thank you for your consideration." Because that didn't sound all kinds of weird.

"I needed to eat as well. We have the vanilla ice cream we bought along with some strawberries and the pastries to make strawberry shortcakes."

I grinned. "My favorite."

"Yeah, I remember. You look tired."

"I'm exhausted."

"Then shower or take a bath or whatever, and I'll have the food ready."

"Okay." I started toward the house.

Stormy was hard on my heels.

I pivoted to turn back to Noah. "Is this okay?"

"She missed you today, and no amount of me telling her that you were coming back would persuade her not to be sad."

I knelt. "You were sad? You barely know me."

Stormy licked my cheek.

"You might just wind up being her person." Noah grinned. "Which just means I'll have to rescue my own dog."

"You're going to recreate your menagerie."

His face darkened. "I never should have moved in with Leroy. What a disaster that proved to be." He'd had to re-home a cat to move in with the cheating creepoid. It had broken Noah's heart, but Fluffy—the name she'd come with—had wound up in a home with three other cats where she'd quickly taken the reins and had decided she needed to be top cat.

No one—not human or feline—had argued. Yeah, she'd landed well.

And Noah was now alone.

I'd considered asking if he wanted to see if the family would be willing to let Fluffy go so we could bring her to California, but I figured Noah'd known that was an option. If the cat was as settled as we'd been led to believe, then taking her back would've been stressful. Not to mention a car ride across the country. "Well, Leroy is in the rearview mirror. Let's head inside."

A slight breeze wafted across the lazy spring day, but heat still lingered, even as we neared early evening.

"Shower then grub." He patted me on the back. "You did good."

We walked together up to the house and then ascended the stairs.

"How do you know?"

He cocked his head. "You're you. Truthfully, you wouldn't give less than a hundred and ten percent. Dillon's lucky to have you." He opened the front door and held it so I could step through.

Stormy followed with Noah bringing up the rear.

The house was marginally cooler, but he hadn't been running the a/c in the last bit of time, so heat again lingered.

I headed upstairs. In my room I sniffed my clothes as I stripped. Not stinky—so I could wear them one more day. I'd need to run over to the closest town that had a discount clothing store because I needed way more jeans and T-shirts. A week's worth, at least, so I wasn't doing laundry too often. The well was deep, but I'd heard about drought conditions persisting in California, and I didn't want to use water if I didn't need to.

And on that thought, I didn't linger in the shower, even though my muscles would've appreciated a soak. Instead, I cleaned myself and hopped out. Then I dried off, donned a distressed T-shirt and sleep pants, and headed downstairs.

Noah would understand I didn't want to get changed a second time. Nope. I'd eat, maybe watch half an hour of television, then crash. I was exhausted—physically and mentally.

"Sit." Noah gestured toward the table. "Unless you want to eat in front of the television."

"Nope, this is perfect." Sometimes we crashed and ate in front of the boob tube. My favorite times, though, were when we sat and just chatted about our days. Whenever he was single, I ensured we spent as much time as possible together. When he was in a relationship, though, he tended to lose himself in the guy and, as often as not, forget about me.

No, that was too dramatic. Just...I'd have to fight for his attention. That hurt.

I plopped into the chair and sighed.

Noah placed a huge bowl of salad before me. "That bad?"

"Like the day we went climbing in the Ozarks."

"Ouch." He placed a glass of chilled lemonade by my hand. "That was something we never repeated."

"I know, right? We're fit, but that trek was insane. Well, today sort of felt like that. But I'll get used to it, and I'm not complaining, okay?" I dug my fork into a slice of cold chicken as he sat next to me with his glass of ice water and his dinner.

He put the creamy peppercorn dressing by my hand.

I took it with a grateful smile and doused my salad. Then I picked up the fork with the chicken—now covered in dressing. Just the way I liked it.

We consumed the first few bites in silence.

I eyed Noah. He had something on his mind, and I was damn curious. "You find any new clients today?"

"A few people visited the website, but no calls yet. I did go over to Hartsville to put a flyer up in the pet store as well as to talk to the manager about offering lessons. He seemed open to the idea, but said he needed to talk to the owner. If it's a go, we'd have to decide if the store would offer them and pay me or if they'd just sponsor the classes and I'd be responsible for everything."

"That's great news." I speared some lettuce. "Anything else interesting happen?"

"The manager, Sam, sort of asked me out?"

"Is that a question or a statement?"

"Uh...both?"

"Are you going to go out with him?" *Please say no. Please say no. Please say—*

"I don't think so." He dipped a piece of chicken delicately into his dressing. "He was damn attractive. Dark, flawless skin. Big brown eyes." He glanced down at Stormy. "Not like hers, but puppy-dog eyes nonetheless." He sighed. "And brawny. Totally didn't wonder if he could haul bags of dog food around."

"Oh. Well, attractive is good." *Here we go again.* Noah had a *type.* Somehow, the good looks always covered up a major flaw—usually that the guy was a jerk. "Are you sure—" I speared another piece of lettuce. Perhaps harder than was strictly necessary. "—that you're ready for another relationship? You're barely out of the last one. And you kind of got your heart broken. Maybe take a break before diving back in?"

For all I knew, this guy might be *the one.* I might be talking Noal out of the perfect relationship for him. Yet I couldn't stop myself. "I mean, maybe if you wait a month or two? Until you're settled? He lives over in Hartsville, so that's a long way to go."

"Actually, he lives close to Foggy Basin and commutes. He just loves animals that much."

Oh dear God. "Well, maybe you are ready—"

"Nope. You're right. I can see that now." He pointed his fork at me. "How about you?"

"Me?" I blinked. *Is he asking if we might go out? That he might finally—*

"Did you meet any nice women today? You must've been introduced to plenty of the store's customers. Any attractive women? Did you make them laugh? Might they be attracted to you? Mission Find Christian a Girlfriend has not been abandoned."

Oh dear. I'd sort of hoped he'd forgotten about that. "How was Stormy today? Did you do training? Do you think she'll be able to help with the puppy class? Just over a week, eh? Has everyone paid?"

He eyed me. "I see what you're doing."

"Yeah, asking how your day went. I'm not going to date any woman who works at the store or anyone who might shop there."

Noah pointed his fork at me. "Probably almost every woman in town shops at the store. It's a little unrealistic to say you won't date any of them."

"It isn't if I want to keep my job." I took a sip of the lemonade—enjoying the bite. "Have you fed Stormy?"

"While you were in the shower and don't change the subject."

I blinked, attempting to feign innocence. "I have no idea what you're talking about."

"Oh, I bet you don't." He pursed his lips. "Operation Find Christian a Girlfriend is swinging into full gear next week."

"Oh yay."

So not.

Chapter Six

Noah

I found three clients who wanted personal lessons at their homes. Needless to say, I was happy to oblige. I discovered three dogs desperately in need of a firm hand and, by the end of the first lesson, I'd convinced each of the owners I could whip everyone into shape.

Three happy people signed up for more lessons.

Stormy settled into our home nicely. Although she was my shadow during the day, as soon as Christian came home, she followed him around. During his two days off, she didn't leave him for a moment.

He'd never seen such devotion before and, at first, found it overwhelming. Eventually, though, he settled into the role of being Stormy's *person*.

I was fine with that. In fact, I was already casting a wide net for another dog to add. I didn't want Stormy to be lonely, of course. Not because I desperately wanted a dog of my own.

The next week flew by and, soon enough, I found myself facing ten identical black lab puppies.

Bear, I recognized, of course.

Glynnis had a tight grip on him.

I'd struggle to identify Tibby, Pepsi, Smudge, Frankie, Roxy, Haggis, Bruiser, Penny, and Sleepy. Well, maybe not Sleepy. Initially they'd called her Bette—but with her penchant of dropping to sleep all the time, I understood why they'd changed the dog's name. She certainly wasn't a firecracker.

"The vet says she's perfectly healthy." Flora, Sleepy's lovely owner, assured me. "She's just...not very energetic. We've had to lower her caloric intake a bit since we don't want her to put on too much weight. I mean, she's happy to go out and play and everything...she just tends to, when not actually walking, curl up and fall asleep. Weirdest thing."

"Kind of like narcolepsy?" I'd never heard of this before.

"Well, narcolepsy is when they get super excited and they fall over fast asleep. Sleepy finds a spot to curl up before gently dozing off." Flora shrugged. "Given the rambunctious nature of my twin six-year-old boys, I hoped to find a dog who would tire them out." She eyed the other nine puppies.

All of whom were excitedly pawing at each other, nipping each other, trying to climb over each other, or—in the case of Penny—surveying the entire group like they were just a little out of their minds.

She'd always shown way more maturity than her high-spirited siblings. Or so her owner reported. Daphne, Penny's owner, clearly had a keen sense of all things dog.

Pepsi and Smudge, named by an enthusiastic five-year-old and a sarcastic twelve-year-old—their father's description, not mine—were all over each other with lots of nips, yips, and growls.

Had I been the breeder, unless these were the last two, I would not have put them together.

The sarcastic twelve-year-old, Brooke, and her overwhelmed father, Richard, were the two designated people responsible for the dogs. Richard was eager. Brooke?

I was going to have to win her over.

Frankie had a shock of white fur on her chest and the cutest yowl when something displeased her—which happened often. Mickie, her owner, confessed she might have three cats in the house and apparently Frankie now thought she was a cat, and wasn't it great her *silly* dog could be around dogs again?

I had my doubts—Frankie really did have an impressive yowl that sort of did sound like a cat.

Tibby's owner, Soren, was a handsome man with a shock of white hair and not a wrinkle to be found. So, either the hair didn't match the biological age—which was entirely possible—or he had freakishly smooth and unlined skin.

I wasn't certain which, but I was definitely curious.

I was also concerned about Bruiser. Clearly the dog had all the inherent gentleness one could expect of the perfect lab puppy. His owner, a stick-thin and short man named Junior was clearly hoping the dog would compensate for...something. He wanted a big, strong, bruising dog. He'd adopted a marshmallow.

Duncan's Haggis was big, strong, and man, did that dog have an attitude. I'd have to watch her carefully while also nurturing her spirit. The man was self-effacing, adorable, and reminded me of Christ-ian—slender with red hair. While Christian's eyes were this amazing shade of green, though, Duncan's were crystalline blue.

Roxy was a spitfire, but her owner Janelle was in control. The woman used to train service dogs, but she'd retired from that work.

She totally could've trained Roxy on her own, but she liked the idea of socializing the puppy.

I worried she might know more about training than I did, but she assured me up front that she wasn't here to judge—just to get some of the zoomies out of her beloved pet.

"Okay." I used my outdoor voice—which worked because we were, in fact, outside. Most of our lessons would be out here. The family room at the back of the house could accommodate a fair number of people, but I'd want the dogs farther along in their training. Accidents were inevitable, but I preferred to have as few of them as possible in—

Bruiser squatted and, within an inch of Glynnis's foot, pissed.

"Oh dear." She scooted out of the line of spray just as her Bear decided to nose his way up Bruiser's butt and, yep…

"Let me get a towel." Realistically, Bear needed his entire snout washed, but I wasn't going to worry about that.

Glynnis merely shrugged and gave me the *what can you do* look.

I appreciated that. "Okay, everyone pay attention to me."

Well, Penny did.

"Puppy class is as much about socializing and teaching good manners as it is about actual commands. By the end of the class, though, you should be able to loose-leash walk your dog, and they should be able to sit, come, and wait." I surveyed the mass of wriggling bodies. "Any questions?"

"Will you have potty-training hints?" Mickie eyed Frankie. "Had to be my favorite Manolos."

I winced. I didn't even want to think about what *that* cost her. "I do have potty-training hints. Let's save them for the end. Now, I want to introduce Christian and his dog Stormy. She's about nine-months-old and, as you can see, fairly well trained. I'm going to show you a few things she can do so you'll know what's possible." I eyed Janelle, who smiled back. As a former trainer, she certainly knew what any given dog could accomplish.

Christian took Stormy through a series of basic commands and, to my relief, she nailed every single one.

For today, I started the class on working through *sit*. Which, as always, proved hilarious.

Sleepy nodded off, and nothing Flora did would interest the puppy who would crack an eye, yawn, and put her head back on her paws.

I nudged Christian. "Can you see if Stormy might get Sleepy interested? Clearly she's over her siblings." I wasn't certain I blamed her even as Tibby and Frankie started tussling. "Let's separate them. We've got playtime coming up."

As I hoped, Mickie took Frankie a few steps away while Soren attempted to wrangle Tibby into a sitting position. I couldn't help but notice how nice his ass looked when he bent over.

Yum.

Haggis steadfastly refused to sit—or do anything except stand with her head cocked—like she was trying to figure out what Duncan's problem was. As if her owner was the problem, and not her.

Typical.

Labs were generally amenable, but they could also be incredibly stubborn. Haggis was a prime example of this.

I showed Duncan how to guide Haggis into a sitting position and then when to reward her. Each owner had a pocketful of treats, and I was encouraging the proper dispensation of them.

Janelle had Roxy well in hand, so I moved on to Daphne and Penny.

Penny, for her part, was sniffing a particularly fascinating patch of grass. She might be the most mature of the bunch—which really wasn't saying much—but she was also the most curious. Clearly very scent-driven.

"Okay, why don't we try guiding her?"

Daphne sighed. "I just love her enthusiasm. Since my divorce, I've wanted to get a pet. My ex was allergic, and so I couldn't have one. Now I'm alone again, it felt like the perfect moment."

"Divorced?"

Her blue eyes flashed. "Oh, not like that. We were just better off as friends. I'm glad we didn't have kids, though, because I believe, whenever possible, kids should have two parents. But not if they're making each other miserable."

"Did you marry young?" *Okay, way too personal a question…but she doesn't look more than about thirty.* "Sorry, that was rude of me."

She waved me off. "Twenty-two, which felt like a good time but, in retrospect, we should've waited. And perhaps if we'd waited, we never would have married. I never saw myself being divorced at twenty-nine."

"Oh, you're not much older than Christian and me." I gestured to Christian who had, to my gratitude, awoken Sleepy from her slumber.

The puppy was playing with Stormy, who appeared quite amused with the game.

Not a lot of *sitting* going on, but I could worry about that later.

"Really?" Daphne's gaze tracked over to Christian and, as if seeing him for the first time—or at least in this new light—she licked her lips. Then she returned her attention to me. "Glynnis says you're new in town."

"Yes. I was so lucky to run into her at the feed store." I gestured to the group. "My first class. Well, here in California, anyway."

"I want to pin the accent as Southern."

"Tennessee."

"Ah."

"Christian has the same accent. Although his voice is smoother than mine. He's got this great soothing tone that can lull the most stressed person. And his nature is very soft."

"Soft?"

"Well, considerate. He's always putting other people's feelings before his own. I'm hoping he'll find someone who will honor that."

Daphne eyed me. "You're not a couple?"

"Oh, no. I'm gay and he's straight. Best friends for twenty years, but not lovers."

She arched an eyebrow. "Are you trying to encourage me to ask him out?"

"I'd never do that." *Backpedal. Fast.* "I'm just extolling his virtues."

"You sound like you're trying to find someone to date him."

I cleared my throat. "Oh, I think Pepsi's about to lose a gasket." So was twelve-year-old Brooke, who really was too young for this. But each puppy needed a handler, so this was what I had to work with. Not ideal.

"I'll think about it." Daphne eyed Christian. "He is very cute."

Instead of trying to sell him further—because, yeah, that had been a bad idea—I headed toward Pepsi and Brooke.

Thirty minutes later, after a short attempt at leash training along with a play session where all the puppies piled into the center of the training ring—except Sleepy who was, of course, asleep. By the time class was over, several puppies had to be carried to their cars.

As I gave Mickie some potty-training tips, out of the corner of my eye, I caught sight of Daphne speaking to Christian.

Frankie kept trying to gnaw on Stormy's leg.

My dog would, gently, bop the puppy on the head. She might've still been a puppy herself, but she had a good grasp of pack behavior—which would stand us in good stead as we progressed through the various classes.

Mickie and Frankie departed as I continued to surreptitiously watch Daphne and Christian.

"Do you mind if I ask a question?" A soft, masculine voice pulled me from my observations.

I pivoted to Soren and offered a broad smile. "Of course."

Tibby, as if sensing this was an important moment, sat and gazed up at me.

"How can I help?"

His light-brown eyes sparkled with amusement. "She's proving to be a handful."

"Ah, lab puppies should come with a warning label."

"My last dog was a boxer. He did come with a warning label—I just didn't heed it."

"Ah." I chuckled.

"I loved him. Truly, I did. But he was definitely the...dumbest...dog I've ever had. I also miss him terribly."

"They do have a way of worming into our hearts." I eyed Tibby. "A boxer to a lab's a bit of a leap."

"I was looking for a placid dog. Clearly I wasn't reading the right forums." He gazed down. "I adore her, but this is the most placid she's been since I brought her home."

"Maybe you and Flora could trade dogs. She was hoping Sleepy would tire her boys out. Clearly the dog has no interest in doing that."

Soren chuckled. "If I thought I could talk Flora into it, I might've considered it. At first, at least. Now? I'm kind of attached."

Tibby, again as if sensing the moment, started chewing on Soren's shoelace.

"Stimulation. You need to give her your full attention with lots of toys and games. Keep that mind of hers moving so she can't get up to mischief."

"Mischief is the right word. She's a whirling dervish. I turn my back for ten seconds..." He shrugged. "I didn't really need that umbrella anyway. My fault for having left it on the bench."

"They can be good chewers. Puppy-proofing your house is critical."

"Oh, I know. I never unproofed it during my entire tenure with the boxer—that would've been dangerous. The umbrella was a moment of lack of concentration." He leaned in. "My brother was trying to hook me up with this guy. The guy's cute, but totally not my type. But how am I supposed to explain that to my brother? He wants to be supportive, but doesn't understand, uh, things."

I eyed him. "Yes, dating gay guys can get complicated."

His face brightened. "Right? I hoped you'd understand."

"Oh, I do. Christian has tried to set me up a few times, and I was like, uh, no. Just...no."

"Top?"

"Yep."

"And he's tried to set you up with other tops?"

"Yep. Bossy ones at that." I couldn't believe I was having this conversation with a puppy parent, but I was in need of someone who understood. "He's convinced *the one* is out there for me somewhere." I sighed. "And here I am, trying to set him up."

"Daphne's a great woman. She was honest with us about her newly divorced status. If I knew someone to set her up with, I totally would. She's got a wicked sense of humor."

I smiled. "That's great to hear. Christian's a bit of a dark horse. He can come across as quite serious sometimes—" Even as I said the words, he and Daphne burst out laughing. "Well, okay, then. Clearly they've discovered their senses of humor."

Soren nudged me. "Who knows? Maybe they'll bond over dogs. I'll head to the pet store and buy more toys."

"Try some food puzzles as well. Tibby's young, but she's food motivated and clever—she might take to them quicker than you think."

"Got it." He pressed a hand to my arm. "Thank you."

Instead of being disconcerted by the unexpected grasp, I was touched. I hadn't had any physical contact with anyone since I left Leroy.

Well, except the amazing hugs Christian gave me whenever I seemed to need them.

I met Soren's gaze. "See you next week." I bent at the waist and stroked Tibby's soft fur. "You be good."

She blinked up at me with enormous dark-brown eyes.

Yeah, I think this might just work.

Chapter Seven

Christian

Do not ogle Noah's ass while he's bent to pet the puppy.

Right. Like a stern lecture from my inner voice was somehow going to have me paying attention. Uh...no.

"So you've really never gone strawberry picking?" Daphne offered me a smile. "It's actually a ton of fun. We should go next month. They grow in the late spring."

"Uh, sure."

"Christian?"

Something in her tone of voice had me refocusing. "Sorry. Strawberries. Spring."

She smiled, with sparkling eyes. "Soren's gay. Just inserting that into the conversation."

I frowned.

She countered with a grin. "You can't take your eyes off him. And I can completely understand. I was so disappointed when I found out he doesn't swing my way. I mean, I'm fresh out of my divorce, and probably shouldn't be looking, but I'd have to be blind not to notice him. Premature gray and owns it. I love that confidence. I figure I'll be coloring my hair as long as I'm able—I don't ever want to show my age."

Does she realize Soren and Noah are probably setting up a date right now? They make a striking couple—

"Christian?"

I blinked. "Daphne, I'm so sorry."

Stormy bonked Penny on the head again.

"Hey." My dog gazed up at me with completely innocent eyes.

Penny resumed trying to mouth Stormy's paw.

I'd have sworn to God that my dog rolled her eyes as if to say, *kids...what can you do about them?*

She truly was a precious dog.

"What I can't figure out—" Daphne gazed between me and the two men. "—is if you're interested in Soren or Noah. Because either presents interesting options. Oh, or maybe you like both, and you'd like a ménage."

My eyes widened. "It's not like that."

"If you say so." Her eyes sparkled in a way that assured me she didn't believe my denial. Like, at all. She pressed a hand to my arm in a very informal, but not unwelcome, gesture. "Life's short. I don't regret my marriage or my divorce. But I'm not going to sit on the sidelines. Obviously, I won't hit on either of those two men. Or you," she quickly added. "That said, any of you might be bi..."

I was about to try to deny I was gay. Or even make a feeble attempt at claiming to be bi. The truth? I was gay. And I had feelings for precisely one man. "I'll do better at concealing it." I offered a smile.

"Or you can own up to it and tell the truth. Life's too short for regrets." She squeezed my arm. "Okay, you've inspired me."

I blinked. "I have?"

"Yes." She said the word definitively. "I'm going to make a profile on one of those dating apps."

"Uh..." *Seriously? That's what you got from this conversation?* "Are those things even safe?" I flashed back to the three jerks Noah had met through various apps—including Leroy the creepoid.

"Of course." She pursed her lips. "But I promise to tell someone where I'm going and with whom."

That only made me feel marginally better. "I wish you luck. I'm good, though, okay? No need to say anything to anyone."

"Ah, so, Noah. The man must be blind—living with you and not even noticing. Still, I'll keep quiet. But if you get together, I'd like to know about it."

I met her gaze.

"So I can gloat." She gently tugged Penny's leash. "Come, Penny."

The puppy perked, clearly understanding playtime was over.

Noah didn't intend to teach *come* until later in the class. Unsurprisingly, Penny would be ahead of the curve.

"Don't wait too long." With those parting words, Daphne gently urged Penny to follow her.

Soren appeared to be ending his conversation with Noah as well. He gave me a quick wave before heading to his car. He was, objectively, a very attractive man. Who, as Daphne suggested, wore his prematurely gray hair with grace and dignity.

She suggested that, had their positions be reversed, that she'd color her hair.

I wasn't certain I wouldn't do the same thing.

Noah snagged the poop bag discarded at the corner of the ring—because wow, could Bruiser produce some stinky shit—and he headed my way.

I cleared my throat. "Soren seems nice."

My best friend halted his walk. "Sure."

"He's gay."

"I'm aware."

"Well, I'm just saying maybe you should ask him out. When puppy class is over, if there's a conflict. Although I'm not certain there is. It's not like you're going to give Tibby preferential treatment or better grades because you're dating her daddy."

"That's true." Noah gestured for us to walk toward the gate for the pen.

Stormy fell into step with me.

"Right? So you should make a move."

Noah halted. "Last week you said I wasn't ready for a relationship and I shouldn't go out with the pet store manager."

Shit. "That was different."

"How?" He held my gaze. "Because I'm trying to figure out, aside from the fact you've met Soren, and not Sam, why things have changed in the past week."

Shit. "Well, I have met Soren. He seems nice." *And it'll break my heart, but I want you to be happy.*

"Christian?"

"Yes?"

"I'm going to ask you a really important question."

"Okay."

"Are you suggesting I ask Soren out because he's white?"

My eyes widened. "No. Not at all. I'm suggesting you ask him out because he seems like a nice guy." I floundered. "You always seem to pick jerks." I wanted to point out there were plenty of nice Black men...but that he never seemed to pick them. Instead, I opened my big mouth and said, "Can you just get over your distrust of white guys?"

"What the fuck are you talking about? I don't have a distrust of white guys." His brow furrowed, and he appeared truly confused.

"Yes, you do. You only ever date Black guys. Why is that?" *Oh God, do you really want to step into this? This is such a fraught subject.*

Yeah, but if he keeps on this trajectory, I'll never stand a chance.

Do you really have one anyway? You're being selfish.

"Because I'm only attracted to Black guys." Even as he said the words, his brow furrow deepened.

"No, you're not—because you point out cute white guys all the time, but you only ever date Black guys. And creeps at that. There are plenty of nice white and Black guys, but you never seem to pick them." *In for a penny...*

"That doesn't mean anything. I don't understand where you're going with this."

"You have a hang-up from all those losers your mum dated." Along with Noah, I'd watched his mother date her way through a series of not-so-great men. I adored Mrs. Gainey, but she didn't appear to believe she deserved a good guy either. I worried Noah was following in her footsteps. But how was I possibly going to convince anyone they deserved better when I couldn't even stand up for myself?

"No, I don't." He gestured. "Jesus, Christian, where is this coming from?"

Frustration welled within me, and I spat out, "You don't trust white guys."

He rolled his eyes. "Of course I do. I trust you. You've been my best friend since forever. Whatever you're thinking, it's just wrong."

"No, you don't trust me."

"Yes, I do." Exasperation was clear in his tone.

"No, you don't. Because if you trusted me, you would've believed me the first time I told you Leroy was cheating." *Careful where you go with this.*

Yeah, but I'm tired of playing it safe.

"You never told me that."

"Yes, I did! You dismissed it—you said, *they're really good friends.*" I let out a long sigh. "And then when I told you again, you dismissed me, saying you trusted him. In the end I had to send you—" *Shit. Shit. Shit.*

Noah's eyes widened.

The silence stretched between the two of us.

"What the actual fuck, Christian." His voice was very quiet.

I knew what that meant. "Shit." I blew out a breath. "I was never going to say anything—especially when you left him. I mean, he was cheating on you. And I worried about whether he was being safe. Whether he was risking your health. And you'd given up Fluffy to be with him, and he so didn't deserve you. Wasn't worthy of you, and then he cheated. I tried to tell you. That I'd seen them together, and they were way too...friendly...to be just...friends." *When I say that out loud, it sounds extra stupid.*

Yeah. Except my instincts were right, and he was cheating.

Noah tossed the bag of dog shit at me.

I caught it easily.

"I'm going for a very long drive. I don't know when I'll be back. Take care of Stormy." Then he stalked away.

That he felt he had to ask me to take care of our dog hurt more than the bag of dog shit being tossed at me.

I watched as he got in his car and drove to the road. Props to him, he got out of the car and closed the gate before getting back into his car and driving away.

Stormy whined.

"Sorry." I leaned over to unclip her leash. "Do you want to go for a walk? We could walk the property line."

Storm clouds had moved in overhead, but the meteorologist had said the rain and wind would come later in the afternoon.

After tossing the bag in the garbage, I clicked my tongue and headed toward the outer fence.

Stormy followed.

In the end, the weather forecasters proved wrong, and we were at the far end of the property when the rain started. This wasn't a gentle downpour either. In one moment, we had a light breeze and then next we were in a torrential downpour.

My dog, who apparently still didn't like storms—for very good reasons—bolted ahead for the safety of the porch.

I considered sprinting but, in the end, decided I deserved to get soaked and cold.

When I reached the house, Stormy nudged against me. Which was the perfect end to this clusterfuck—I was going to end up smelling like wet dog. I led her into the house and dried her off as best I could. Then, once she was settled on the bathroom mat, I took a shower.

When we were both drier, we headed downstairs. Since it neared dinnertime, I fed her.

The rain continued to pour down in buckets, but no thunder or lightning accompanied it, so Stormy appeared okay with the noise.

I checked the crock-pot to find the ribs nearly cooked. I'd planned ahead so we'd have something hearty to share after the first class.

All that effort had proved to be for nothing if Noah didn't return home. Well, I'd leave a plate for him in the fridge, but that wasn't the same as fresh-out-of-the-crock-pot ribs.

By seven, I was clearly not going to have company for dinner. I ate the ribs, fresh corn on the cob, and mashed potatoes—all Noah's favorite foods.

The entire silent meal, I cursed my stupidity. For bringing up every sore spot in Noah's life—including a few he might not've even known he had. *Although Aunt June admonished me many times when I put myself down, I couldn't help myself then, and I still can't help myself now.*

If Noah tried to put himself down, of course, I argued vociferously. He was a damn smart man. And yeah, full-time college had been out of reach, but he'd still spent all that time learning to train dogs. Between his talent and what I'd learned at business school, we had enough to make a success of his business.

Yeah, but will he ever want your help? I should put everything I do in writing so he'll know what needs to be taken care of.

I thought about the pens we planned to buy. The doggie daycare we considered opening. All the training classes Noah planned on teaching. If I left, he wouldn't be able to afford this place on his own. He needed me.

Just like I needed him—and not just because of the money. I'd heard of some rooms. Over the local watering hole? Somewhere I could go and probably survive on my salary.

Noah couldn't survive without me right now.

Unless he went to Soren and they're going at it right now. Or the guy from the pet store. Or he installed an app, and—

I needed to stop. I could spiral downward fast when I started thinking of Noah with his hookups. With his boyfriends. All those nights he assumed I was out with Laura—but was actually home alone. I'd assumed Laura was home alone as well.

She'd always been tactful. She'd also let me know she wasn't ready for formal courting yet.

I'd trusted that she knew what she was doing and that, when the time was right, we'd come out with our engagement announcement.

God knew, our parents were putting enough pressure on us.

Well, more, my family. They needed the money. They needed the share of the company that the Frankstons were going to gift me upon my marriage to their daughter.

I still resented my parents. They'd overspent for years and when facing bankruptcy, had sold thirty percent of their share in the business to the Frankstons. So instead of the fifty-fifty our grandparents had created, we were now minority owners in the business. A continuously growing business.

Still not enough for my parents.

When I married Laura, the Frankstons planned to gift me twenty percent—which my parents planned to take possession of immediately.

What a mess.

A *clusterfuck* as Noah liked to say.

Since I never swore, I stuck with *mess*.

I climbed into bed with a weariness I hadn't felt for a long time. Even when we'd put in those long days driving across the country, I didn't feel as tired as I did tonight.

When Stormy leapt on the bed to keep my company—against Noah's rules—I didn't have the energy to shoo her off.

Or maybe, just as likely, I wanted the company.

Sleep was a long time coming.

But come it did.

Chapter Eight

Noah

I came home that night. I was still right fucking pissed off. But I came home.

Partly because I had nowhere else to go and not enough money to waste on a motel for the night.

Parly because I missed Stormy.

Mostly because I didn't want to worry Christian.

Because he'd worry. He always worried about me. Up until today, I'd taken that for granted. Now, though, I needed to be more aware of it. Need to be careful of how that affected our relationship.

I heated the ribs and ate them while standing at the breakfast island. I expected him to come down and admonish me at any moment about eating properly—sitting so I could digest the food. Or some other stuff he was always carrying on about. Stuff I often questioned. Like, did I really digest food better while sitting down? And, while I was on that track—who had given him that advice? If he told me a medical journal, then I'd give it due consideration.

If he said his mother, I'd likely toss the advice. Mrs. Carter might come across as a nice person, but I didn't trust her. She and Mr. Carter never had Christian's best interests at heart. I knew way more than I should have about the whole Laura debacle. I'd never share with my best friend how I knew what I knew—more that I needed to watch out for him.

I was world-weary.

He was naïve and trusting.

Well, except Leroy. He hadn't trusted my ex.

He'd been right.

To my shame.

Which might've been the other reason I'd come home. I wasn't certain I bought the whole assertion about me only dating Black men or his logic about my mother. Or at least I didn't agree with his underlying assertions of the reasons why we did what we did. Had I dated only Black men? Yes. Did my mother stick to white men? Yes. Did we both pick abysmally? Yes, to that as well.

So, should I be giving Soren a second look? I suspected we would compatible—in bed, at least. And he loved his dog more than life itself. That definitely counted more than looks or employment or anything else that someone might consider important. That said…he was a damn attractive man. Just…not for me. Even if Tibby wasn't in my class, I probably wouldn't go out with Soren.

Where does that leave me?

I scraped the bones from the delicious meal into the compost and then headed to bed.

In the morning, I had fewer answers and more questions.

Christian, ever the chipper morning person, sat at the kitchen table, Stormy loyally at his feet, while eating eggs, whole-wheat toast, strawberry jam, fresh orange juice, and coffee.

I headed to the pot, snagged my extra-large mug from the cupboard and poured a massive cup of java.

Finally, he gazed at me. "Can I make you some breakfast? I can make an omelet, some toast, and maybe fry up some bacon."

"I'm good."

He scowled. He never approved of me mainlining caffeine rather than having a nutritious breakfast.

"I can get my own food." I cleared my throat. "But thank you for the offer."

"At least a piece of toast with some peanut butter? Protein to carry you through until you eat a full meal?"

This was a debate we had every morning. And every morning I relented. I snagged the white bread and put two slices in the toaster oven. When I went to grab the peanut butter from the shelf, however, I discovered the jar was already on the table. Because of course it was—he knew I'd give in and have the protein he carried on about.

As soon as the toast popped up, I plated it and headed to the kitchen table. I sat in my regular spot—right across from him.

I sipped my coffee.

Just do it. Rip off the bandage. Put everything on the table. Let the chips fall where they may.

I was certain I could come up with more trite expressions, but none were forthcoming. Finally, I slid my knife through the butter and applied the slab to my toast. Way more than I needed—which always pissed off Christian.

He's worried about your cholesterol. At least someone is.

Yeah, I didn't care, and neither had my mother.

She wasn't a bad mother...just inattentive. She left me alone with my animals. She could've forbidden them, so that was something.

Next, I slathered the peanut butter. The crunchy kind—which was my favorite. And we always had some in the house, even though Christian preferred smooth.

Guilt gnawed at my gut. He did so damn much for me, and I didn't show nearly enough appreciation. Still, he'd overstepped yesterday, and we needed to hash this out. "Why'd you do it?"

He looked up—his startled gaze meeting mine. He swallowed, looked away, then looked back. "Because I love you."

I shook my head. "What?"

His green eyes didn't flicker.

"What are you talking about?"

"I love you." He ate a forkful of eggs.

I sighed. "I love you too, but you destroyed my relationship." I eyed my toast. "Yes, Leroy was cheating. We always used protection—" *I was pretty sure.* "—and we were doing okay. I mean..." Except I didn't condone cheating. That's why I'd left his sorry ass—and Tennessee—behind.

"No, I mean I'm *in love* with you." He took a bite of his toast.

A drop of strawberry jam dropped onto his plate.

If that had been me, it would've landed either on the table, or more likely, my shirt.

I repeated his words in my mind. He said it casually—as if he hadn't just dropped a nuclear bomb on my world. Yet...maybe I'd misunderstood. "But you're straight." Because that would change the equation...right?

"No. Not really." He took a sip of juice—acting as if we always discussed his love for me.

"But you were going to marry Laura." Again, with the logic. Because I had to find something to grasp onto. Something that would make this...less believable? More believable? I couldn't be certain.

"Yes." He used a spoon to scoop up his jam and ate it.

My mind whirled. "Oh, my fucking God. You just *went along* with marrying Laura to get your parents out of debt?"

"Yep. Pretty much." He eyed his coffee. Whatever he saw had him rising and heading to the coffee pot.

"You need to stand up for yourself more! Jesus, Christian. Marrying her would've been a huge mistake. And for your parents? Those ungrateful sods? Who never gave you the time of day unless to figure out how to use you?"

"Why?"

I blinked. "Why what?"

"Why do I need to stand up for myself more?" He dumped the remnants of his doctored coffee down the sink, ran the water, then proceeded to pour a fresh cup.

"Why? Because you end up doing shit you don't want to do. If you like guys, fine. I'm happy for you. But you have to say what you want. You have to do something to get it. You can't be a doormat." *God, is this why he came to California with me? Because he just goes along to get along? Because he doesn't know how to stand up for himself? How the fuck had I never noticed that?*

He poured a ton of milk into his coffee and started heaping the artificial sugar in as well. He really preferred lattés, but he couldn't always get to the nearest café or coffee shop. "I don't like *guys*. I like you."

"I'm sure you're confused about that." On inspiration, I repeated the words he'd asked me a few weeks back. "If you could do anything, go anywhere, what would you do?"

He held my gaze. "I'd live with you and all your dogs that you surround yourself with to try to make yourself the family you never had. In other words, I'd do exactly what I'm doing now." He squinted. "Except I think we need to get another dog or two. And maybe some rescue cats? I put my foot down at ferrets, though."

"Uh, I'm going to visit Pam at Safe Haven Animal Rescue. She's got a pair of mutts. They got dropped off last week. Best Pam figures, the purebred breeding mama got knocked up by someone other than her stud, and when the breeder realized, she offloaded the puppies as quickly as she could."

"That's horrible." He pressed a hand to his chest. "How can people do such shitty things?"

"Well..." I considered. "We'll take Stormy. If she gets along with the puppies, then we can probably bring them home in a day or two. They've had all their shots, and they're fifteen weeks old, so they're ready to go."

"They're just a little bit older than the lab puppies."

"Yeah, just about."

"Well, that's perfect. You can demonstrate on a puppy, and I can take part in the class as a participant."

"So you can spend time with Daphne?" Jealousy reared its ugly head until... "Never mind. Soren's more your speed, right?"

He chuckled, but without true humor. "Noah, you're my speed."

"But what about when I'm ready to date again? Are you going to be okay with that?" Because although I wasn't attracted to Soren, there might be other guys out there who would scratch an itch. Or, if I was really lucky, be willing to build a life with me. Of course, if someone moved in here then Christian might feel he had to leave.

I'd feel horrible.

He smiled. "No. But it doesn't matter. You need to understand—I've loved you for twenty years. I'll just keep on loving you in whatever capacity you want me."

I rolled my eyes. "Oh my God, Christian, that's ridiculous. As your best friend, we need to sort you out." Because in no way could he be *in love* in love with me.

He blinked. "*Sort me out*? What does that even mean?"

Inspiration hit. "I know! I'll find you a date. A guy. Now I know why all those girls bombed with you." I couldn't be certain this was why Laura eloped with someone else—but the relief I'd always felt at him not being chained to her magnified. Maybe my subconscious had always known he was gay. Or maybe I'd just known, in my heart, how detrimental—how soul-destroying—that marriage would've been.

"Uh." He scratched his clean-shaven jaw. "So, you're not mad at me anymore?"

Own it. I took a deep breath. "I had a lot of time to think yesterday. Yes, you were wrong to do what you did. I mean, it was sort of illegal."

"Nothing *sort of* about it. If a cop had come along, I would've been arrested."

God save me. "Okay, well we have to agree you're never going to do that again. However—" I took a deep breath. "—creepoid was a creep. I'm sorry I didn't listen. Now we're going to get you a date and get you over this crush you think you have on me." Because that absolutely felt like the right thing to do to get us out of this mess.

He cocked his head. "Noah, it's not a crush."

Of course he just had a crush on me. I wasn't a person someone as perfect as him could ever love.

Which is maybe why you keep picking losers.

Whoa. Wasn't going to touch that with a ten-foot pole. "I'll find you a date." Because this was something I *could* do. "Now, how about

Soren?" I laughed. "And here I thought you and Daphne would make a cute couple."

"She's a lovely woman...but no. Definitely not. And besides, I don't know how to date. I mean, I've only ever dated Laura. And, truthfully, that was more just going to obligatory events together. Real dating? I'm clueless."

Okay, confirms he's really lucky Laura ran off with the other guy. "Fine—we'll double date then."

Again, he blinked. Sort of owlishly. Super cutely. Like he needed glasses, even though he had perfect vision.

"Are you willing to try a date with Soren? He'd be someone very gentle to start with and, who knows? Maybe you'll hit it off."

"I don't think this is a very good idea."

"Trust me, it will be fine." I picked up my toast. "After we see Pam about the mutts, then I'll call Soren. Now, we need to find someone else."

"Oh dear."

Your expression doesn't give me much hope, but trust me...I'll make this work.

Because I somehow had to.

Chapter Nine

Christian

The drive to the Serenity Animal Rescue in Hartsville took a bit of time. Dealing with Pam Scholls, the director, took longer. The woman was in her early fifties with blonde hair. She was also on the shorter side and truly had a...strong...personality.

I liked her.

"I called your references." She held Noah's gaze. "Your old boss was really sorry you left in a hurry." She arched an eyebrow.

"That's on me." I raised my hand. "I just needed to get out of there. See, I was supposed to marry this nice woman—Laura. And she ran away with someone else, and everyone in town was assuming she'd broken my heart and was treating me with kid gloves. That's so stifling, right? You know what I mean. So, one day I asked Noah that if he could do anything—live anywhere—what would he do? He said Foggy Basin and a dog training business. I said we had to leave the next day. I might've implied I'd leave without him, which I totally wouldn't have. He was between training groups, and is there ever a good time to pack up your life and move? Anyway, we, uh, did."

"Did?" Pam blinked.

"Did move across the country. We're from Tennessee, in case you couldn't tell. The accent sort of gives it away. Although some people guess like Georgia or Alabama. I guess the southern accent sounds the same to everyone out here, right?" I grinned.

She glanced between the two of us, finally settling back on Noah. "You've taken a lease on the house for a year?"

"Yes."

"So you're not just going to take off suddenly and leave the dogs behind?"

"Absolutely not. Stormy is our first rescue, and I'll admit I was thinking an older dog—like a senior—but you told me about River and Sable and...my heart kind of melted." He shot me a look, which I interpreted as *please shut up, you're not really helping*.

Admittedly, I wasn't a great liar, and I'd sort of told three or four half-truths in that monologue. Well, one-quarter truths. I ran through the words in my mind as Noah and Pam sorted the paperwork.

Okay. Several flat-out lies.

I winced inwardly.

But all that really mattered was that Noah got the puppies. Of course, he'd be the best owner ever—that was a given. Naturally he'd be able to give them the best home in the world—how could that be in doubt? Stormy and I were just a bonus.

Speaking of... My girl sat in the heel position by my leg and waited patiently. She'd been so excited to go for another car ride. We had a tether system for her so she could see out the window. We had two crates to bring the puppies home in.

When the nice other lady, whose name I totally missed, brought the two puppies out, my heart exploded.

They were smaller than the lab puppies, even though they were a couple of weeks older. They had light-brown-and-cream fur with weird markings.

The woman handed one to Noah.

His face immediately relaxed and transformed into the biggest, brightest smile. "Hello, Sable." He pressed his face to the dog's. "I'm going to give you the best home ever."

She licked his nose.

Stormy pressed against me.

I petted her. "You'll get your turn."

Noah pivoted to us and slowly crouched. "Stormy, this is Sable. Be gentle."

The warning was a nice touch, but my girl didn't need it. She nosed the little dog and then licked her nose.

Sable let out a tiny yelp.

My heart melted.

Noah repeated the process with River.

Pam looked on with approval.

Forty minutes later, with the puppies secure in their crates, we headed for the pet store.

Dollar signs flashed before my eyes. *You still haven't told him about the money.* Right. He had no idea I'd squirreled away every penny I'd earned basically since the day I went to work at the family firm as an intern.

Mr. Frankston insisted all employees—even family members—be paid a living wage. So, I'd been earning decent money since I turned sixteen. More, when I'd been promoted to a junior executive role upon graduation from business school.

I might've let my parents think I was frittering the money away. In truth, I'd opened a bank account at a branch of a big bank in the next town over. Quietly, every two weeks, I transferred most of my money there. I'd invested conservatively, but wisely. Almost ten years of hard work had earned me a nice nest egg. And I'd sort of neglected to tell any of that to Noah.

He'd had to pay for much of his stuff over the years. He could have the pets—as long as he took care of them and paid for them. Vet bills were high, and anytime he managed to get something saved, one of his animals would get sick. That was the peril of owning pets. "I got my first paycheck on Friday." I had Stormy on a short leash as I pushed the cart through the store.

Noah had a puppy under each arm and, as I'd silently predicted, every single person we'd run into wanted to see the puppies.

One woman had brazenly asked Noah over for a *puppy playdate*.

I didn't have anything against great Danes, but that dog could've squished one of the pups. *So could Stormy, so watch out*.

Noah gently declined the offer.

"I've got enough money. I haven't spent my entire last check from the credit union, and I have the tuition money from the lab puppies as well as the three private clients." He fingered several collars. "I don't want to do traditional blue and pink."

"Agreed."

"So navy-blue for River and purple for Sable?"

I eyed the two bundles. "Well, we definitely need a way to tell them apart. What did the vet say she thought they were?"

"He. Dr. Malcolm Jones. We have an appointment in two hours at his Fluff & Tuff Animal Clinic back in Foggy Basin. Pam's best guess is a terrier mix. I'm thinking there's some Japanese Chin."

Although I tried to keep up, many of the breeds eluded me. I trusted Noah to prompt me if any knowledge was crucial. Knowing what these two were would be somewhat important.

He grabbed two collars as well as two matching leashes before tossing everything into the cart. "Why did you lie to Pam?" He tossed the question off casually, as if asking me if I wanted more sweetener in my coffee.

Spoiler alert—the answer was always *hell, yes*.

"Lie?" I might've squeaked that.

He eyed me. "That word vomit thing you did. Which is really not like you. Getting you to discuss anything personal is like pulling teeth, and all of a sudden, you're giving a stranger your life story."

"Well, not my *entire* life."

He offered me a raised eyebrow.

"Just the Laura stuff. Which was all true. Everyone in town pities me for being stood up. I mean, we weren't anywhere near the altar, but everyone assumed we were. Everyone assumed I was heartbroken—even though I totally wasn't." *Then you started dating creepoid...that broke my heart.*

"Still. You didn't have to make it sound like I *had* to follow you."

"Do you think they need raincoats?"

"With the drought? Not likely. They'd grow out of them in thirty seconds anyway. We can figure that out in the fall—months from now." He pursed his lips. "But they will look super cute if, when they're full grown, we buy them matching coats."

I leaned in and petted each of their heads in turn. "Hear that guys? You're going to be so cute." I made the cutesy voice I knew drove Noah nuts.

He groaned.

We finished shopping, he paid, and then we loaded everything in the car for the drive back to Foggy Basin. We arrived at Fluff & Tuff just in time, and we were escorted to the exam room immediately.

The nice tech weighed our two new ones.

"Oh, we should get Stormy weighed as well." I gestured to my girl.

Paxton had paid for a vet visit for her when she first arrived, and she was in perfect health, so she had a few more months before her first birthday check-up.

"Great, let's step into the lobby." The technician eyed Stormy. "She's not going to fit on the little scale in here."

We all laughed as I guided her to the much-larger scale.

She sat pretty, and the tech noted her weight, then compared it to a month ago. "That's another seven pounds. She's growing like a weed."

I flashed to the two puppies. "She'll stop eventually, right?"

"Yes, I promise. But she's going to be well over one hundred before she stops." Another gentle smile. "Why don't you head back into the exam room? Dr. Jones did Stormy's check-up a month ago, so he'll be better able to give you an idea of what you're facing. I'm so glad she got rescued—she's such a sweet dog."

I petted her head. "She's just perfect."

"We thought so. Hard to believe someone abandoned her."

"Horrible thing to do. Except if they hadn't, I wouldn't have her, and she's just the best girl." I snuck her a piece of kibble.

She licked my hand.

The technician laughed and guided us back to the exam room.

Where I expected to find Noah alone, I discovered a super-handsome guy in a lab coat who was laughing uproariously with my best friend.

The two were a matched set—dark skin, laughing dark-brown eyes, and mirrored grins.

Noah spotted me first. "Oh, Christian, perfect timing. Malcolm was just telling me about the time, as a kid, that he..." He trailed off. "Are you okay? Is something wrong with Stormy?"

I had no idea what my expression actually was...but apparently whatever it was prompted Noah to be concerned. "Uh, Stormy's fine. Malcolm?" I might've squeaked that.

The taller man, who was about my height, extended his hand. "Dr. Malcolm Jones. I'm not as formal as some vets are." His gaze lowered to Stormy. "And how are you, precious girl? I hear you've found your forever home."

Something in his tone had me relaxing.

A fraction.

The way he was so casual with Noah rankled. I couldn't have been gone more than a few minutes.

I smiled. "Forever home is right. She's just precious. And so smart. She already knows so many commands. And Noah's teaching her tricks. Maybe you can tell him about that?" I gave Noah *that* look.

He cocked his head.

Sable yipped.

Noah and Malcolm laughed—again at the same time.

"Puppies don't always appreciate being ignored. Let's take a look at these. I saw in their chart that the vet over in Hartsville examined them a couple of days ago, when they were first dropped off. She didn't note anything on the file, but I appreciate you bringing them in so I can give them a thorough exam." The vet gently stroked Sable's soft fur.

"Well, you're going to be their vet. So, we're going to be getting to know each other quite well." Noah was all grins.

I managed a smile.

Barely.

By the end of the exam, I could admit to being impressed. I knew nothing of vets and exams and all that stuff—those had always been things Noah had to deal with—but the way Dr. Jones handled the puppies was damn impressive.

Noah was just placing them on the ground when he pivoted his attention to the vet.

Okay, I thought we were finished.

"So, Christian happens to be single..." Noah glanced my way.

I shot daggers back.

Dr. Jones pivoted his attention to me. "I wasn't going to ask, because I sort of got the vibe you were together—"

"Nope." Noah answered quickly. "Just two gay best friends who are new in town and looking to meet people. Christian agreed to let me set him up—"

Oh hell, he did not just go there.

"And being his best friend, you're obliging him?" Dr. Jones smiled. "Dating a patient's parent isn't encouraged, but one dinner won't hurt. I'm newer in town and am always up for a good time helping to welcome newcomers." He met my gaze. "If you're all right with this."

"Fine." I plastered on a smile, all the while trying to figure out how I could murder Noah and get away with it.

"Great!" Noah beamed. "How about tonight? No sense letting grass grow under our feet."

The favorite expression of our ninth-grade physical education teacher as he pushed us to do *yet another* twenty pushups.

I always hated the guy.

Even as these thoughts circled in my mind, I hatched a plan. "Blue Star Diner okay?"

"I love them. Can't wait." Dr. Jones offered me a wide grin with perfect teeth.

My gaze shifted to Noah.

Better sleep with your door locked.

Chapter Ten

Noah

"I cannot believe you did this." I hissed the words at Christian as we entered the Blue Star diner.

Together.

Because, apparently, we were on a double date.

The hiss might've been more effective if I didn't have to angle my head up to reach his ear.

Tonight, I was going to be the shortest guy at the table. Which really didn't matter.

Right. Keep telling yourself that.

Malcolm, Christian, and Soren were all a smidge over six feet.

I was well below.

Right. Soren. Because somehow Christian got a hold of the guy's number, and the next thing I knew, I was being blackmailed into a double date.

How the fuck did this happen?

Oh, right. You had the bright idea that setting Christian up would absolve you of all the guilt you feel about having totally missed that he's been in love with you for the last twenty fucking years.

Yeah.

That.

"For two?" Gabriella greeted us with a smile. "Nice to see you again."

"For four." Christian offered a shit-eating grin. "Double date."

"Oh, that sounds like fun." She led us to a booth near the back. "Who should I be looking out for?"

"Dr. Jones, the vet. He's such a sweetheart." Christian fluttered his hand.

Oh, for Christ's sake, you don't have to go over the top.

"And Soren Johansen. Tall? Cute?" More fluttering—only this time his eyelashes. Seriously, he looked like he had something caught in his eye.

"I know Soren and Dr. Jones. I'll definitely send them your way." Gabriella deposited the menus on the table.

Despite my best efforts, Christian managed to get me to slide into the booth first—trapping me between him and the wall. I growled.

"What would you like to have to drink?"

I wanted to ask for a beer. Instead, I asked, "Could I have a cola?"

"I'll take a sweetened iced tea." Christian's unrelenting grin wouldn't quit.

"Sure. Back in— Oh!" She waved.

I checked over Christian's shoulder and, great, Malcolm and Soren were walking our way. Both men wore grins to match Christian's.

Fan-fucking-tastic. Everyone's happy here except me. Not wanting to be the grump to everyone's sunshine, I plastered on a smile.

The men paused at the end of the table before Soren slid in, clearly having figured that since he and I were on the *date* that we should probably sit across from each other. "Nice to see each other in a less-formal setting."

Malcolm laughed. "Do you run your puppy classes like military training?"

"That's hilarious." Christian chuckled. Just a little too loud. A little too forced. "Noah's classes are great fun. He's so good with the dogs. I can't believe we had to leave ours at home tonight. But we tuckered them out, and they were asleep." He turned his attention to Soren. "We got two puppies today. We were told they were mutts—"

"Definitely some Chin," Malcolm added.

"Right? Somebody surrendered two adorable puppies. I just knew Stormy needed a younger sibling. Who knew we'd pick two?"

"Who knew?" I echoed the words, trying to inject some enthusiasm.

Christian nudged me. "Show Soren that cute picture you took of them. Oh, no, wait."

I hadn't actually made a grab for my phone—which was in my back pocket—before Christian had his out.

"I took this of Noah when he was asleep."

"You what?" I slept mostly naked, so I might've been panicking a bit.

"An hour ago. You remember? Well, you were asleep, so obviously you don't remember." He tapped, swiped, tapped again, then handed the phone to Soren.

Who grinned. "Okay, that's a great photo."

"May I see?" Malcolm gestured to the phone, but held Christian's gaze.

"Of course." My best friend bobbed his head like a freaking bobble doll.

Malcolm took the phone from Soren and his face took on a dreamy quality. "That is one to cherish." He handed the phone back to Christian.

"May I see?" I arched an eyebrow.

"Uh...sure."

I hadn't been naked an hour ago, so that wasn't a worry. More like wondering if I'd been drooling while... I sighed. I sat on the couch, with a puppy under each arm, and my eyes closed. I hadn't realized I'd drifted off to sleep. And I certainly hadn't been aware of him taking my photo. Of feeling compelled to do it. Which raised the question of whether he had other photos of me. I eyed him.

He snatched his phone back.

Ha!

Okay, so I'd have to steal it from him at some point and delete all the bad photos of me. *To what end? What's the true harm?* I didn't have an easy answer to those questions.

"Soren, I'll bet you don't know that Noah has an uncanny ability to predict storms."

I rolled my eyes. "It's called a weather app."

Christian kicked me under the table.

I tried not to wince. Then I plastered on a smile. "Malcolm, you won't know this, but Christian can greet you in nineteen different languages."

Malcolm's eyes widened. "That's really impressive. Which languages?"

"Mandarin, Swahili, Ukrainian, Portuguese—"

"One cola and a lemonade." Gabriella placed the drinks before us. "And you gentlemen?"

"I'll have a coffee, if that's okay." Malcolm smiled. "Long day. Need a pick-me-up."

"I'll have one as well." Soren smiled. "Only make mine decaf."

The other three of us at the table groaned.

What was the point of coffee without caffeine? Seriously.

"Does everyone know what they'd like to eat, or do you need—"

I grabbed the menu. "I'll have—" I scanned quickly. "—the chicken pot pie."

Christian arched an eyebrow.

I glared.

Okay, except I don't love chicken pot pie. Should've ordered the chicken fingers. Oh, fuck it—chicken is just chicken.

He shrugged. "I'd love to have a cheeseburger. Keeping it simple."

Malcolm grinned. "You know I love the meatloaf with extra gravy."

"Sure do." She pivoted her attention to Soren. "Soup of the day is tomato basil. A bowl of that and a side Caesar?"

"Perfect, thank you."

I tried for a smile. When one came to a diner, one should enjoy greasy, unhealthy food. Tomato basil soup? With a salad? What was he, a rabbit?

"I'm watching my fat intake. I've had some liver issues." Soren shrugged. "Nothing too serious."

"Oh, that can be concerning. Although the liver is the organ most able to heal and regenerate. That's why someone can give half their liver to a donation and be fine." Malcolm turned to Soren. "What have your liver enzymes looked like?"

Soren launched into some long explanation about a certain test and how it had something to do with...

Nope.

I was totally lost.

Christian leaned over. "He's so cute."

"Then maybe you should date him." I rolled my eyes.

"I thought you wanted me with the vet."

"Right. Sorry. Lost track of the plan."

"And I've got everyone's meals." Gabriella slowly unloaded her tray with the most heavenly smelling food.

We thanked her and turned our attention to consuming food. Compliments about the food before us and general comments about the town were exchanged, but everything felt...off. Like I should've been doing more.

Chicken pot pie might not have been my favorite, but the thing was damn good. I inhaled as the uncomfortableness of the situation continued.

Soren was clearly a nice guy, but just not someone I was interested in. He worked from home as some kind of computer specialist security something. I noted that if I ever needed computer help and Christian wasn't around, I might just call Soren. Likely wouldn't be able to afford his rates, though.

Christian finished his burger and wiped his mouth. "Okay, so that was the best burger."

"Even better than Big Burger back home?" I'd yet to try the burgers here, but the diner back home was amazing.

"Truthfully? Yeah. And since I'm never going back to Tennessee, I don't have to worry about offending anyone."

I cocked my head. "What do you mean you don't intend to ever go back? You'll see your parents, right? And I suppose if Laura ever comes back, you might want to see her. To hash things out once and for all."

"Uh... No. I care for Laura like a friend, but there's nothing to hash out. She ran away with Thad. Who's a good guy, so I don't blame her. God knows, he was a better choice—"

"She didn't know you were gay."

"Well, that's true, I suppose. But I think if I told her I was gay, she wouldn't be entirely surprised. Look, she's a nice woman—and I wish her well. But she's my past, Noah. You're my future. I mean, obviously not as a partner, because you're not interested in that. But as the person I care about. Who I want to be with. And if that means platonically living together in the house and dating other people, I'm totally fine with that."

"I'm not." I wanted to stomp my foot. "Women flocked to you—at least until they found out you were basically engaged—"

"I was never engaged—

"—basically engaged." I repeated the words to remind myself that up until yesterday, I'd thought he loved Laura and had felt betrayed by her departure. It hadn't really entered my mind that he might've only wanted friendship with her. Come to that...what had their physical relationship been like? Had they been intimate? If not, had Christian taken male lovers in the interim? While waiting for me to get my head out of my ass. I could see now, as of this morning, that he'd laid his feelings on the line. I didn't reciprocate them—but that fact had consequences. He'd date other people. He'd find someone and want me to move out or he'd move out or his lover would move in and—

"Noah, I can see the gears grinding in your mind." He smiled. "Why don't you let it go and just enjoy tonight? We are sort of on a date."

At once, we both turned to face our dates. Of course, talking only to Christian had been the height of rudeness—but we had a lot to still hash out.

And found the bench across from us empty.

"What the hell—"

"Did you guys want to order dessert?" Gabriella appeared out of nowhere and offered menus. "Or perhaps a coffee? Although the caffeine—"

Christian raised his hand.

She stopped talking.

"Uh...did our dates both go to the washroom? At the same time?"

My mind flashed to all the things two guys could do in a bathroom, superimposed Malcolm and Soren in those images, and I cocked my head. Because that made a compelling visual—even if just in my mind.

"No." Gabriella said the word slowly. "They both asked for their slices of apple pie to go, paid for their meals, and left together. Oh." She brightened. "Dr. Malcom said to wish you both a good evening and Soren added you make a lovely couple. I didn't realize you were together, because you said you were just friends—but he's right, you make a cute couple."

My mouth dropped open. Our dates had abandoned us? Had left together.

"Clearly neither of them found either of us appealing." Christian chuckled. "Can't say that's ever happened to me before."

"Uh, me either..." *What the actual fuck?*

"So, dessert...?" Gabriella still held the dessert menus.

"Apple pie with vanilla ice cream." I managed a smile. "He'll take apple pie with chocolate ice cream. Don't ask."

She shrugged. "I won't, but I think he's got good taste. Everything tastes better with chocolate ice cream." Then she was gone.

Christian tapped the table with his index finger. "Are we supposed to call to apologize?"

"I have no idea. They're the ones who got up and left. Were we really talking that long?"

"Uh...I'm clueless. I mean, they could've said something...right?"

"I suppose." I tried to replay the conversation in my mind. Where I'd wanted Christian to commit to always being with me. But I hadn't said the words out loud. Or at least I didn't think I had. Because, if I had, that would've sounded really bad.

Gabriella arrived with our scrumptious apple pie and we consumed all of it before finally gazing at each other.

He was so dear to me...but I didn't *love* him. Not in *that* way.

Right?

The answer, which would've come so easily just a day ago, didn't.

Chapter Eleven

Christian

Noah sat, nibbling on his toast while I'd barely touched my eggs. Last night's debacle still hung heavy in the air.

I'd texted Malcom to make sure he was okay. Well, under the pretext of a wellness check. He'd apologized, saying something about an emergency. I hadn't assessed him as a guy who might lie, but that didn't mean he'd been truthful.

Soren had popped off a quick text to Noah, saying how he'd left Tibby alone too long and how he'd needed to get home. Okay...sure... But why not at least say *goodbye* before taking off?

The guys' actions made me wonder if maybe they'd hooked up. If they'd found in each other what each had clearly found lacking in Noah and me.

I was especially peeved at Soren. He'd looked at Noah and found him lacking? Lacking in what? Noah was damn near perfect. Hell, most of the time he *was* perfect.

How do I move us past this impasse? He's looked at me a couple of times this morning. Is he seeing me differently? Can I take advantage of this? Is pressing forward the right thing to do, or should I be backing off?

Fuck it. "I've never kissed a guy before—can you show me how it's done?" I sipped my coffee.

Noah's gaze shot from his toast to mine. "Could you repeat that?"

"Well, I've never kissed a guy before." I shrugged casually. "Can you show me how it's done?" In truth, I'd barely kissed a girl either. Laura and I had exchanged a couple of attempts—like if we could somehow make out, then we could make our relationship work. *How'd that work out for you? And you think it'll be different with Noah? He's got to* want *you—he doesn't right now.*

Sometimes I hated when my inner voice was right.

Noah cocked his head in that way I found so endearing—like he was trying to solve some great puzzle of the universe.

Only this time, things were entirely simple. I wanted him. Would do anything for him. Hell, I'd moved across the country so he wouldn't be alone. Now, some of that had been self-interest. Getting away from my hometown, the Frankstons, and—most especially—my parents, had been critical.

"Christian?" His voice croaked a little—as it often did so early. He was definitely *not* a morning person.

"Hmm?" I took a sip of orange juice.

"You say you love me?" His nose did that little wrinkly thing I found so endearing.

"Yep." The congealing eggs really needed to be eaten, but Noah's dark-brown eyes held me mesmerized.

He cleared his throat. "Like in a sterile, non-sexual way?"

Truly adorable. "No. Not at all." My toast, with strawberry jam, was slightly more appealing, so I bit into that.

He eyed me. "So...? If I said I wanted to take you to bed right now? You'd just agree?" Dubiousness permeated his words.

Be honest with him...even if your first inclination is to jump up and down and yell, 'hell, yes'. I took a breath—and also a moment to compose myself. "Well, no. I'd first ask you what you meant by that, because I'm a virgin, and therefore I don't think I'm ready for you to fuck me through your headboard on the first night. I need to work up to that." I tilted my head, as if in consideration. "But I might be wrong about that."

He gaped. "About which part? The *I'm a virgin* part, or the *fuck me through your headboard* part? Because I have to say..." And then he didn't say anything. He opened and closed his mouth several times, but no actual words came out.

Finally, "You're.... a v-virgin?"

I enjoyed how he stuttered the last word. "Yep." Said with great enthusiasm. "But if you want to make me a non-virgin, I'd be very happy to cooperate." A grin split my face at the idea of doing all those firsts with Noah. Because as much as I saw him as my best friend, I also wanted so much more—intimacy, caring, and affection. I wanted him to love me the way I loved him.

"Uh.... I think I need to think about this." He drank several mouthfuls of coffee.

"Okay. Take your time. There's no rush." Because I didn't see him kicking me out, and I certainly wasn't going to turf him. I was sort of relieved things hadn't worked out with either Soren or Malcolm last night.

Noah blinked. "Oh my God. You're so not bothered about this, are you?" His pupils were again wide as he clearly tried to sort out the conundrum that was me.

"I love you. I will take as much or as little as you're willing to give." To me, things really were that simple. Really were that black and white.

He squinted in that way he did when he was thinking really, really, really hard. "And if I said I wanted you naked in my bed in three minutes and I *was* going to fuck you through my headboard, you'd go along with it?"

I grinned. "But you wouldn't say that to me, Noah. I'm not one of your boyfriends. However, if you're willing to show me how to give a blow job, I'll go for it." Because that idea intrigued me as much as the first day I'd realized that was a thing—probably way earlier than I was supposed to. What could I say? I had a very creative imagination—especially when it came to coming up with ways to be intimate with Noah.

There's that word again. Because, to me, this was so much more than just body parts coming together. To be a broken record...I *loved* him.

He let out a long breath. "Jesus Christ. Fucking Hell. You can't just say that sort of stuff to a guy and..."

I batted my eyelashes. "And...?"

After several attempts at coherent speech, he just spluttered nothing that made any sense.

So I took control of the situation. "Fine. I'll just sit here and watch my eggs congeal while you make up your mind. I start late today because the fresh-fruit shipment is arriving at three, and I need to get it all put away. Just to let you know, I'll be a bit late home tonight. Go ahead and have dinner. I baked a lasagna yesterday, and it's in the fridge, you can heat up a slice—"

"You really have never given a blow job?"

I hesitated. I could play this several different ways, Cheeky, serious, or honest. "Have you really never received a blow job from a white guy?" Honest always won.

"I'm not sure that's the point I'm trying to make." He pursed his lips. "It will be, like, a first for both of us, then..."

Yep, honest earned me brownie points.

"You'll show me?" I downed the rest of my coffee.

"I've never been with a guy who hasn't...you know..."

I arched an eyebrow. "Never been with a virgin? Well, this will be virgin territory for both of us."

He groaned.

As I expected him to.

"Do I just get on my knees?" Because logistics were a thing. If I crouched between his spread thighs...but then I still needed to get his pants down. Could I...?

"Christian."

"Hmm?"

"This is a big leap."

"You don't want a blow job?" I batted my eyelashes.

"Uh, is there a right way to answer that? Because most guys are not going to turn down a blow job."

"Right. Well, no time like the present." I pushed back from the table and made my way to him. I yanked his chair, that scraped on the vinyl floor but luckily didn't leave a scuff mark.

"Hey." His eyes went wide.

I grinned as I sank to my knees. "This is going to be so much fun."

He groaned. "This is such a bad idea. We need to talk about...shit."

"Blow job now. Talk later. Seems pretty simple to me." And it did. I just needed to get him in the mood. Despite having known him for twenty years, I didn't really know what got him off. He'd mentioned porn once and how it hadn't gotten him *excited*. Personally, I hadn't thought that was a bad thing—but that was just my puritan family roots being exposed.

I preferred to be with someone and focused on them, rather than what might be on the screen. Mind made up, I grasped the tab on his zipper and attempted to pull it down.

He laid his hand over mine. "Christian." A hoarse whisper.

"I want this, Noah. Have wanted it forever." I gazed into his dark-brown eyes. "Maybe you didn't know—"

"I didn't."

"Well, you do now. If you want me to stop, of course I will. But I just want to bring you pleasure. That doesn't seem like a bad thing."

He blinked. "It's not. I'm just not certain I want your first time to be on a kitchen floor."

"I swept up the dog hair before you arrived."

Speaking of dogs, our three were happily hunkered down, with Stormy being covered by River and Sable. They each had their own bed, but somehow, they were all on my girl's. They'd all slept in my room last night—given how late Noah returned, that had made sense. Would we split them up tonight? I didn't know.

"Sweeping and making breakfast? Somehow, I think I should be giving you a reward."

My insides lit at his words—so he understood the intention behind the blow job. A reward. For him coming home. For us working through our differences. Not everything, to be sure, but much of it.

Slowly, he guided my hand to lower his zipper.

I grinned.

He held my gaze with an intensity I'd never seen before. Or I certainly didn't remember seeing it before.

When I tried to pull down his boxer briefs—with an idea of liberating his, uh, cock, he rose a bit so he could yank them down over his hips.

Need to clean that seat. He might be newly out of the shower, but my little neat-freak heart knew what it wanted. Dog hair everywhere? That I could live with for a day or two.

Bare butt on the vinyl of a kitchen chair? Nope, that had to be cleaned.

He pressed his finger to my frown line. "I promise I'll clean it up." He pulled down his briefs, and his erection sprang free.

I licked my lips.

He chuckled. "Eager much?"

"Now I've decided on a course of action? Yes, I'm very eager—" I gave him a lascivious smile. "—and I think you are too.

"It's been... What?"

"I'm not sure I want to hear about the last time you were with creepoid—"

He barked out a laugh. "You think Leroy ever gave me a blow job? Uh, yeah, that would be a hard no. Not his style. He liked to fuck and then promptly fall asleep—whether I'd gotten off of not.

Does that mean Noah would bottom for Leroy? And what the fuck is no blow jobs? *Isn't that a natural part of a relationship?* I really didn't want to dwell on creepoid, so instead of focused on Noah's gorgeous cock. A little on the big side—compared to mine. I didn't have a lot of experience with this.

Actually none, but what did that matter?

I hadn't snuck peeks at the guys in the locker room. I'd been all about getting in and out as quickly as possible. Team sports weren't really my thing.

And that's enough thinking about things that aren't relative.

Gently, I traced my finger along his length. Soft and smooth—which wasn't a surprise. Mostly flaccid—which was disappointing.

Yet, as I made a second, and then a third pass, his cock twitched.

A third and fourth sweep elicited a moan *and* a thickening shaft.

I took him in hand and gently squeezed—adding just enough wrist action to give a little twist.

"Yes." He hissed. "That. Again."

Emboldened, I repeated the action.

He grew even more in my hand.

I grinned. "Now?"

After meeting my gaze and holding it for a super long time, he nodded.

I got to work. I licked a drop of precum from his cock, even as he held himself still. As he grew harder and harder in my hand. "Yum."

He chuckled.

Finally, I sucked his crown into my mouth.

His cock twitched.

Figuring that must mean I was doing something right, I swirled my tongue around the head as I pulled him deeper and deeper into my mouth. I grasped the base of his cock as I tried to bring more and more of him into my mouth.

And nearly gagged.

Great.

His hands on my cheeks gently guided me back, even as humiliation swept through me and heat rose in my cheeks.

"Christian?"

"Hmm?"

"Can you look at me?"

Of course I could. I'd never deny him anything. So my gaze slowly rose to his.

"Although I appreciate what you're trying to do, how about we take things slowly?"

I bobbed my head in acknowledgment. Then I tried again. This time, I was careful not to let him touch the back of my throat. Instead, I focused on swirling my tongue around him, sucking hard, and holding him steady.

His hands roamed aimlessly in my hair—alternating between pulling, fluffing, and then just holding still.

Although he was a guy frequently in motion, he could have moments of stillness when nothing around him moved.

"I'm coming, Christian. If you don't want me to come in your—"

I sucked harder.

He jerked and then spurted in my mouth.

I continued to swallow as he filled my mouth. I'd never tasted cum before, so this was a bit disconcerting. On the other hand, it was erotic as hell. My cock strained against my jeans as I tried to tamp down the need rising within me.

Finally I pulled off him, easing his soft cock so it landed gently in the nestle of black curls.

"Are you hard?" He gazed into my eyes.

I nodded frantically.

He yanked up his T-shirt. "Will you come on me?"

Holy hell, you better believe I will. Even as I had the thought, I grasped his knees to lever myself into a standing position. With unsteady hands, I unbuttoned my pants, and slid the zipper down. Then I yanked out my dick and pumped it several times. I barely had time to think about lube before my body went rigid. I erupted and shot cum all over his stomach. A bit landed on his T-shirt, and one rope splashed on his chin. I held in the giggle—but it nearly burst out anyway. I could barely hold myself upright and could only imagine how debauched I looked.

And he looked how I felt—blissed out and satisfied.

"God, Christian, you're so beautiful." Through hooded eyes, he managed to hold my gaze. "I think I always knew, but..." He drew in a lungful of air.

"You don't have to—"

"I mean it." He snapped that. Then winced. "Sorry. A little orgasm-drunk."

I wasn't certain that was a thing, but I held my tongue.

"You've always been attractive. You're hit on all the time."

He's not wrong. So fight the instinct to argue—sometimes it's okay to hear the truth—even if it makes you uncomfortable. "Thank you."

"You think I'm bullshitting you. I'm not. All pale skin, tousled red hair, stunning green eyes. I've always taken you for granted. You're Christian. My Christian. My best friend."

Panic welled within me. "I still am, Noah. Nothing's changed."

With a chuckle, he ran his hands though the cum on his chest and licked his finger. "You tell yourself that."

"I need to get cleaned up." I tucked myself back into my pants and headed upstairs to the shower.

Nothing's ever going to be the same again.

Chapter Twelve

Noah

I sat there, blissed out, for quite some time.

Finally, I grabbed a paper towel from the table and did a passable job of cleaning up. I'd take a shower later. For now, I needed to get out of the house. I whistled, and three pups appeared.

Well, Stormy came immediately, with Sable and River trailing behind.

I gave them my most winsome smile. "Who's ready for training?"

Stormy dropped to her butt and waited for a treat.

"Good girl." I let her lip one off my hand.

Then I gave the hand signal for *sit*.

Of course, I had to guide the younger two into the position. Soon, though, I rewarded them. "Why don't we go out to the training pen?"

Stormy eyed me.

"You'll manage without something every time." I snagged three training leashes and headed out.

After a fashion, Stormy followed.

River and Sable followed as well. Wherever the older dog went, they were quick to follow. That might work for now, but there'd come a time when Christian would want just Stormy, and everyone shouldn't get too attached...

My heart seized at even the idea that my best friend might leave.

What did you expect? That you'd grow old together here? Never meet someone else? That neither of you would, at some point, want space of your own? How ridiculous is that?

I put Stormy and Sable into the *sit* position while I clipped the leash to River and gestured for us to walk.

He balked, instead trying to get back to his sister.

Who ran forward to meet him and to glare at me as if to say *how dare you separate us?*

And you thought getting two was a good idea. I'd never had two, and I figured training them couldn't be that much more difficult than training one—which was, admittedly, the most I'd ever had.

About twenty minutes later, the younger dogs were tuckered out and their attention was completely used up. I placed them in a smaller pen—with a couple of food puzzles—while I worked with Stormy. Whip-smart and eager to please, she was a delight to deal with. That relieved me because I didn't want Christian to grow tired of her. I could manage three dogs, of course, but having back-up felt like something smart to do.

Which circled me back to my best friend.

I put out bowls of water for the dogs.

Is he right? Have I only ever chosen men who look like me? The sentiment felt wrong, but evidence proved him right. I didn't want to delve too deeply, except a pattern was emerging. No wonder Christian never thought he had a chance. He was a nice guy. I never managed to pick nice guys. Maybe I felt I didn't deserve better? Because tons of super-nice guys were out there—I just happened to pick a lot of duds.

A lot of lemons.

I'd never been able to make lemonade. I'd honestly thought Leroy was the one for me. And how fucking wrong I'd been on that score.

After the dogs had drunk their fill, I chose some balls to throw.

Only Stormy understood the concept of retrieving the ball.

Sable and River would catch the ball, then plop onto their bellies and begin gnawing on them.

Super adorable.

"I'm off." Christian yelled the words from the back porch. Then was gone back into the house before I could respond.

My phone sat heavy in my pocket until after lunch. *Call him? Text him? Pretend nothing happened...?* Yeah, that option wasn't likely.

Still, I was in high spirits when Hadrian showed up with Dag for their private tutoring session.

Dagobert, whose name had mercifully been shortened, was a bit of a scamp. The German-shepherd cross was smart, cagey, and had developed an attitude.

My job was to help Hadrian manage the dog now, before the situation got worse.

I left my three in the house—and would likely do that for the next couple of sessions. Eventually, though, I wanted to introduce Dag to other dogs so his manners might improve. Although fixed, he still insisted on trying to mount everything—including my leg. I wasn't, to say the least, impressed.

Still, at the end of the hour, I felt progress had been made.

Well, *hoped* we'd made some headway. Whether Dag was still moving forward next week would be up to Hadrian and how much work he was willing to put into the training.

The rest of the day was uneventful as I pored over my inbox and found a couple of clients had emailed me. I also had a couple of calls—one, a referral from, of all people, Soren. *I owe him a call.* As well, several people were replying to the flyer I'd left at the pet store. Two couldn't make their way to Foggy Basin, so I planned to spend a half day on the road seeing them in their homes. That meant leaving Sable and River at home in their crates. Not the most-fun prospect, but they needed to learn to self-soothe. Plus, their crates were right next to each other. They'd have company and, just as likely, would sleep all day.

Knowing Christian was working late at the grocery store, I decided to leave the leftover lasagna for another day, and I whipped up his favorite stir fry—ginger beef with extra sprouts—and had it waiting for him.

He showered quickly and joined me at the table. His normally burnished-copper hair was a shade darker, since it was still damp. He dug into his food with enthusiasm, so I let him be while I enjoyed my meal as well.

Not shabby. You'll need to do more now he's working all those hours.

Because we were roommates and best friends. People in that kind of a relationship did nice things for each other. I was certain of it.

As he neared the end of his meal, I ventured to speak. "So..."

"Yep." He wiped his mouth with a napkin. "That was delicious."

"What would you like tomorrow night? I mean, we could make a schedule, or I can just wing it."

"I can cook too, you know."

"You're busy at work. You're tired when you come home."

"And yet millions of people cook when they get home—and that's just in our country."

I pursed my lips. "You're still contributing more than I am. I need to find more clients."

"Any leads?" He stacked our dishes.

I stilled his hands. "Yes, but that's not what I wanted to say."

"Well, congrats on finding more people to help." He cocked his head, not pulling away from my grasp.

"Thanks. We can talk about that later."

"Okay." An easy grin.

"We're still not dating. But I was wondering if you'd be interested in learning how to receive a blow job?"

His pupils dilated. Just like that. "Uh, okay..."

"Your bedroom? Or the couch or here or—"

"I haven't swept the floor."

"I can—"

"Let's not lose the momentum, shall we?" Still clinging to my hand, he tugged me up. "My room will be just fine."

We scrambled upstairs, and he had his jeans undone in seconds. "On the bed?"

I eyed the pile of pooches who'd followed us. *Should've crated them*. "Yes, bed might be safest." I pivoted to Stormy and pointed. "Bed."

She went obediently and, as I predicted, River and Sable followed.

Turning back, I found Christian on the bed with a pillow under his head and a very erect cock curled prominently. He'd rucked up his T-shirt, leaving a massive expanse of bare skin, including two nipples, all just begging to be kissed. To be worshipped.

"You're so beautiful."

He rolled his eyes.

Don't roll your eyes at me. Who told you that you weren't attractive? Who made you feel less than? Even as I said the words in my mind, though, I knew.

His parents.

They might not have ever criticized his appearance in front of me, but they'd made other derogatory comments. Like I wasn't even there and couldn't hear. To my shame, I'd only spoken up once.

Mr. Carter had reminded me that my mother worked for him.

I'd learned my lesson—and had always kept my mouth shut after that.

Well, I'll just have to keep telling him how attractive he is until he believes me. I almost pointed out that Malcolm had found him attractive, but that was just a little too weird.

I knelt on the bed and crawled over to him.

He held my gaze.

I lowered my mouth to his nipple and sucked it into my mouth.

He sucked in a breath.

Taking that as a good sign, I nibbled, laved, and nipped the bud.

He raked his nails through my short hair in the way I loved. Funny how he knew that about me.

Slowly, I kissed a trail over to his other nipple—giving it just as much attention.

That elicited another moan.

Satisfied I was making progress—and amazed he'd never had this done to him before—I kissed my way down his sternum to his belly button. He only had a smattering of hair, and I liked how it tickled my skin.

I swirled my tongue in his navel and then moved lower. When I reached his cock, I straddled his hips. This way, I could watch his reaction as I took him in my mouth.

First, though, I licked the drop of precum on his tip.

His eyes took on a dreamy quality that softened the green of his irises in the light filtering through the gauzy curtains covering his windows—that kept out the setting sun.

I tongued his slit before pulling him into my mouth.

He bucked.

I placed my hand on his hip even as I swirled his length around in my mouth. He tasted so damn sweet. I wanted both to savor this forever and bring him to a climax at the same time. Knowing I had to choose, and optimistically believing we might do this again, I grasped his balls in my hands and gently rolled them, all while sucking for all I was worth.

"Uh...um...Christ..."

Cute. Christian never swore, so, for him, that was true blasphemy.

"Noah, I'm coming—"

Was all the warning I got as he spurted into my mouth. I swallowed as much as I could. As I glanced up, and caught him in the throes of passion, I lost focus. I popped off him too soon and—

Yep.

His cum went everywhere.

Everywhere.

Oops.

I wiped my face on the hem of my T-shirt even as he let out a long exhalation and his body relaxed.

"That was..."

I waited, but apparently words were beyond him. So I scooted off the bed, tromped to the bathroom, wet a washcloth, washed my face, and headed back into his bedroom.

Stormy lifted her head in vague interest, but I gave her the *stay* signal. She resettled right away.

Sable and River didn't move a muscle—completely exhausted by the day's adventures. *Okay, so keeping them occupied is going to be the key to having special time with Christian when he comes home from work.*

He'd played with the dogs immediately upon stepping in the door—but had, after about thirty minutes of that—headed for the shower.

Wait...we're going to do this again?

I placed the washcloth on his belly and tried desperately to clean up the mess.

He cracked an eye. "Sorry, I think we may need to practice this one a little more. I came too quickly, and you got it up your nose."

I laughed—likely as he'd intended.

We did try again. After a bit of time. Because refractory periods were a thing.

I might've fallen asleep in his bed that night.

So we won't have to separate the dogs.

Right...just keep telling yourself that.

Chapter Thirteen

Christian

Noah's arms banded around me held me in place even as Stormy sat before me, eyeing me.

"Puppies." I gasped the word, even as I scooted out of Noah's hold and scrambled off the bed.

The smell hit me right away.

One puppy had actually peed on the puppy pad while the other had missed almost entirely.

Despite our proximity to precisely no neighbors, for propriety's sake, I yanked on my boxer briefs before scooping up the wriggling bodies and heading down the stairs.

Stormy was hard on my heels, and I had everyone outside and searching the grass within just a couple of moments.

The back door opened and, as I turned, Noah tossed a bathrobe at me.

I caught it easily and shrugged it on. The air nipped this morning, and my nipples turned to nubs. Nipples Noah had definitely enjoyed nibbling on last night.

Which brought a smile to my face.

"Could you make some coffee? I need help waking up." I had a regular shift today, and after coming home a little late last night, and the blow job, my mind was still a little fuzzy.

"Sure, I can put on a pot." He arched his eyebrow. "Would you like to learn how to give a hand job in the shower?"

I was almost late for work.

In the end, however, I was at work on time, and I greeted Dillion with a huge smile.

He eyed me as if not quite certain what to make of me.

I didn't blame him—I came to work every day with pep in my step, worked my ass off, then went home just as happy. From what I could see, his life was more interesting than he let on. Since that was none of my business, I moved right along.

My week with Noah went much better than I ever could've imagined. More blow jobs, more hand jobs, more sleeping in the same bed.

Except, clearly, he wasn't willing to admit anything more was going on between the two of us. I'd always figured I would be happy being with Noah in a *friends with benefits* relationship. But I wasn't. I wanted more. I wanted way more. I was getting greedy, because as much as I was enjoying the *benefits* part of our relationship, I worried the friendship part might start to slip.

Every day Noah secured new clients, trained our puppies—although Stormy didn't need much work—and every night we came together.

Late Sunday morning, as the lab puppy owners all arrived, I fretted.

Noah was standing with Junior—a clearly anxious Bruiser at their feet—when Soren approached. Tibby was actually walking beside him on a loose leash. I grinned. "Well done."

A bit of color rose in his cheeks. "Tibby's amazing. We do the training in small increments—but do several a day. She's really taken to it." He smirked. "T-R-E-A-T-S definitely help."

"Yes, they're great motivators for the first few rounds of training. Noah's advanced classes work on praise and encouragement rather than food."

Soren nodded. "Don't tell Tibby—she'll be quite upset."

"Generally, the dogs tend to be nine or ten months old before they're ready to start that."

"Will Stormy do that training?" He glanced over at my dog who sat quietly in the heel position beside me.

"Formally? I'm not certain. Noah's already doing most of those things with her all the time. I don't think she realizes she's being trained." I tilted my head. "I've wondered if dogs feel appreciation. Generally it can take a rehomed dog about three months to feel truly comfortable. Trusting that their lives won't be upended again. We're Stormy's third home in her short life—at least that we know of. But she seems to be settling."

"You and Noah appear to be a calming presence in her life." He eyed me speculatively. "And how are things going otherwise?"

Heat crept up my neck, and I knew, from long experience, that a blush was overtaking my cheeks. Damn my pale-skinned ancestors.

"Oh, that's interesting." Soren grinned. "Malcolm and I figured you two should be together—whether you're both smart enough to realize it is another story. Well, let me rephrase. You seem to have figured it out. Whether Noah gets his head out of his ass to figure out what he'll lose if he doesn't make a move, is an entirely different situation."

"He won't lose me." Said quietly and with some ferocity.

"I hope not. I mean, don't pine after the guy forever, by any means. You deserve happiness as well."

"I am happy."

He cocked his head. "Yeah. You have, I don't know, a glow about you."

"Oh look, Richard, his daughter Brooke, and their dogs Smudge and Pepsi have arrived. I should go greet them." I lit out of there like my ass was on fire, even as Soren's chuckle propelled me forward.

Glow? Does that mean he knows what Noah, and I have been up to? Oh God, is it written all over my face? "Hi, Richard. Brooke. How are things going?"

Brooke glared. She had teenager down to a science, even though she was only twelve. Funny how both Noah and I were only children, yet I could recognize attitude so well. Eighth grade felt like a million years ago.

"We're good." Richard met my gaze. "Happy to be here so we can learn more. Smudge is doing great, but Pepsi needs some work."

And since Pepsi was Brooke's responsibility, I wasn't surprised to hear the dog lagged behind her sister.

"Noah's going to review everything from last week first off, and he'll make certain Pepsi's up to speed." Even as I said the words, I noted the pooch was trying to gnaw on her leash. *Oh dear, lots of work there.*

As more people arrived, Noah stepped into the center of the training ring and had everyone make a circle around him. Sable and River were in their crates in the house. We'd bring them out and introduce them to everyone once we hit playtime.

"Okay, glad to see everyone came back." Noah grinned as he surveyed the group. "Anyone want to go first to show me what you've been practicing?"

Janelle's hand shot in the air.

Noah beckoned her to come toward him.

She advanced with Roxy walking loose on leash and glancing at Janelle for her cues.

The puppy did everything on command perfectly and only received a treat at the very end.

She's going to make a great service dog. I didn't know nearly as much about animals as Noah did, but I'd learned enough about temperaments.

We had a woman who worked in the office at the factory who had epilepsy. Her service dog would alert her if a possible seizure was near. We had a safe space for her to lie down and one of us would keep her company. As the person with the most first aid training, that position fell often to me. *I wonder how Ronni's doing. Are the others taking care of her?* She'd caused a momentary hesitation in my decision to leave—but I couldn't stay just for her. I had hopes Marian, our new accounting clerk, would step into the role of...caregiver...? I'd certainly been more than just a junior executive. I'd taken the care of my employees seriously. Way more than my father ever had, that was for certain.

Even as I had that train of thought, Frankie, Penny, Haggis, and Bear all took their turns.

Bruiser managed—but barely.

Sleepy had to be roused, but she valiantly tried.

Smudge aced and Pepsi struggled because Brooke's lack of focus was clear.

Noah was patient, though, in guiding her through some corrections and making suggestions.

Finally, Brooke seemed to be more interested as Noah effused about all the great things that would happen once Pepsi was trained up.

Class continued in some semblance of order as Noah focused on sitting and walking. Only a couple of the dogs managed a loose leash, but that was a goal for the end of class, and we still had some time to get the dogs doing as they were told.

Plus, what toddler ever did as they were told? None as far as I'd ever seen.

By the time the puppies were released into the puppy pile, even Sleepy managed to rouse herself to join the fray.

Noah brought River and Sable out and gently introduced them to the puppies who showed interest. Even though ours were several weeks older, they were much smaller than the labs. I worried they might get trampled, but Noah had everything in hand—as he always did.

By the time everyone left—after Soren had given me *that* look—I was exhausted and ecstatic at the same time. Noah'd been amazing and was clearly in his element. Moving out here was proving to be a really good idea. Although Noah deserved the credit for the idea, I took some pleasure from knowing I'd pushed him into doing it. He never would've come if I hadn't been willing to pull up stakes and move across the country with him.

Noah closed the gate after Daphne and Penny drove away. He sighed.

"You're doing such an awesome job." I grinned broadly. "Even Brooke is coming around, and I can see Pepsi's got potential."

"If Brooke works with her. Big *if*."

"You can always call midweek and say you're doing a check in."

"I'd have to do that with everyone."

I pursed my lips in consideration. "Well, I suppose. Although maybe not—just do it with the clients who are struggling. You're just making certain the pooches are getting everything they need."

"If I can make five calls, then I can make nine."

I did the math in my head.

"I only need to call Richard and Brooke's house once."

"Right." I snapped my fingers.

Stormy bounced over and put herself in the heel position.

"That, my friend, deserves a treat." Noah pointed, then promptly chased after River who was clearly making a break for it. He had nowhere to go, but that obviously wasn't going to stop him as he ran as fast as he could on his tiny little legs.

Sable, not to be outdone, chased after Noah.

Stormy brushed her nose against my hand.

"Right. Treat." I dug into my pocket.

She took the treat gratefully, then joined the fray.

Fifteen minutes later, Noah and I sat on the back porch with three exhausted puppies at our feet. He met my gaze. "Miss Esmeralda at three?"

"Yep." I'd checked with the head nurse this morning, and our landlady was having a good day. We would finally meet the woman. I was excited. She just seemed like such a spitfire. Living here and doing her own thing for more than eighty years.

Noah sort of moved his head in some weird motion I couldn't understand. Was he trying to tell me something? I couldn't be certain.

"We're not dating."

"Right." That pierced my heart, but I'd recover.

"I'm not really interested in you romantically, right?"

"Right." *God, where's he going with this?*

"But do you wanna, like, have dinner with me over in Hartsville at that fancy restaurant?"

Don't shout for joy. It's just dinner. "Uh, sure." *Right. Stay calm. Everything will work out.*

I wasn't certain when my inner voice had become so optimistic—but I'd roll with it. For now.

Chapter Fourteen

Noah

Miss Esmeralda Stanton was a hoot.

No two ways about it.

"So lovely of you two boys to come and visit me." Her distinctive accent wasn't one I could pin down, but she found our Tennessee twang charming.

I wouldn't be sorry if I lost some of that to something more neutral. I didn't like being defined by where I'd come from—I wanted to be defined by my character. By my ability to do the right thing. By my trustworthiness.

Things I couldn't say about many of my ex-boyfriends—or my mother's. So did we pick losers because we didn't believe we deserved better? That appeared to be Christian's theory. I wasn't so certain. Except I couldn't say Leroy had been the exception—because he'd been one in a long line of guys who I'd thought might be *the one* only to turn out to be duds.

"Is he courting you right?" Miss Esmeralda placed a clearly arthritic hand on Christian's.

"Is who?" He gave her a startled look.

She gestured her chin toward me.

"Oh, I'm not—"

"Oh, he's not—"

We both stared at each other.

"Oh hush, you two. I have my ways of knowing things. You've been seen at the Blue Star Diner on several occasions."

I arched an eyebrow. "We're friends. Friends eat meals together at restaurants."

She pointed a finger at me. "That's not all I've heard. Millicent's daughter is friends with Soren's uncle, and he said that Soren said that you two were together." She squinted. "Or that you should be together."

I blinked. Okay, a tad indiscreet on Soren's part...except we had kind of ignored him at dinner last week. And whoever Soren's uncle was...along with Millicent's daughter...? I didn't know any of these people, but I was soon discovering people were the same everywhere. Back home, we'd been in a medium-sized town. All centered around the factory, though, so that made the place a hotbed for gossip.

Knowing Foggy Basin was small—and actually realizing what that meant—made me feel embraced. Yes, I was living under more scrutiny. But I also had people looking out for me. For Christian. That was worth everything.

"He's treating me just fine, Miss Esmeralda." Christian didn't look at me. "The way friends do."

"Friends with benefits, you mean."

My jaw dropped.

"Shut your mouth, my dear, or you'll catch flies. I know what you young ones say these days. And I understand, when one is lonely, how one might choose to have a physical relationship with someone. But you're risking your friendship."

"I would never do that." I had to make her understand.

"See that you don't. Friendship is so important. I had my friend Lucinda—until she passed...a long time ago."

For just a moment, I wanted to ask how close she'd been to her *friend* Lucinda. Except, even if they had been closer, that was really none of my business.

Christian finally met my gaze. "We've only had twenty years so far. I want another sixty or so."

That would take us to eighty-five. I wasn't certain I'd live that long, but I'd certainly give it a try. I also wasn't certain Christian would want me around that long. Especially when he met someone new.

"There isn't anyone else for me." He said the words low—for my ears only.

My chest seized in panic. I couldn't be the man he wanted me to be. He needed to move on with his life and find someone who would appreciate him. Because, in the end, he'd grow tired of me. My mother had. Many of my boyfriends had.

You picked bad ones to begin with. Did that ever occur to you?

It hadn't. Not until Christian had put the idea in my mind. Now I saw the series of train wrecks for what they were—my fault. Partly, anyway. If I'd been more careful—more discerning—I might've wound up with someone special. Someone who cherished me.

Someone like Christian.

I sighed.

"Young man, that was quite a sigh." Esmeralda held my gaze. "Perhaps you need to be cheered up."

"No Miss Esmeralda. I'm fine. Just...pensive."

"Pensive my patootie. You're brooding."

Christian burst out laughing. "I've never heard that expression before."

"Because you're too young, my dear. Now, run along. Did I hear you have dinner plans?"

I sat a little straighter. "Yes, that fine dining establishment over in Hartsville."

"You realize we have perfectly good dining establishments in Foggy Basin?" She narrowed her eyes at me.

"Of course we realize." Christian—always willing to course correct. "It's just that we wanted some privacy—not to have everyone goggling at us through the window. Or even inside the restaurant."

Yes. That. Privacy. No busybodies getting in our business.

"Well, that's lovely. I hope you boys have a wonderful time."

"We plan to." Christian rose, then gathered the lady's hands in his. "I'm so glad we got to meet you. To have you in our lives. I hope we may call on you often?"

"Absolutely. Does this old broad good to see healthy, handsome men strutting around. Keeps me young at heart."

Strutting? Okay...

Handsome I could agree with. Christian's boy-next-door charm came across in spades—aided by the red hair and green eyes.

I waved my goodbyes when the care aide came to settle Miss Esmeralda. Apparently, dinner would be served shortly.

Heading out into the fresh air, for just one fanciful moment, I considered holding Christian's hand. *Ridiculous notion. You're not boyfriends. It's absurd.* Yet it would've also felt right in that moment—I was certain of it.

As we made our way to his SUV, he caught my gaze. "We don't have to go to dinner."

"I know we don't." I grinned. "But I landed six more clients this week—four in Hartsville. I'll be going there for a good chunk of Wednesdays."

"What about the puppies?"

"We can either crate them or set up a space for them and pen them in. Maybe in the family room? They'll be fine—they have each other and Stormy. I mean, they're home alone right now."

He pursed his lips. "I know."

"And it's stressing you out."

He sort of screwed up his face in that adorable way he did when he was trying to make a monumental decision. "Well…"

"They need to learn to be alone. You work. I work outside of the home sometimes. We don't want them to become too reliant on me being home all the time or able to take all three with me. You knew the score when we rescued them—that they'd have to learn to be alone."

"I suppose. You're right, they have each other and Stormy."

We'd put River and Sable in a large wire crate with Stormy loose. We'd also put her bed next to the puppies, and as soon as she got the lay of the land, she plopped onto her bed. Clearly, either at Paxton's or somewhere else, she'd learned being alone was okay.

Once we were secure in the SUV, Christian pointed us toward Hartsville, and I rambled on for almost the entire drive about my new clients, my lesson plans, how I was considering going to San Francisco for some advanced trainer training in about a month, and how I needed to figure out how to get more paying customers.

"You'll work something out." Christian pulled into a parking spot near the restaurant. "You're resourceful." He patted my knee. "You've gotten out of tough places before—and this isn't even a tough place."

I cocked my head.

"You've got me." He grinned. "I'll always take care of you." Then he exited the vehicle.

I'll always take care of you.

Those words swirled in my head as we entered the restaurant. They chased me as we ordered shrimp cocktail appetizers, grilled chicken on a bed of mushroom rice and asparagus for dinner, and peach flambé for dessert.

The meal was phenomenal. The dessert lit on fire truly spectacular. The bill was a little high, but nothing I couldn't handle.

We spoke of inconsequential things. Relived some of the better moments from our past—things I could cling to. I'd called my mother and left her a message that we'd arrived safely. She'd texted back and said to *keep in touch.* Then she hadn't responded to my next two texts. Some days I wondered why she'd had me at all. Except maybe if my father had stuck around then we would've been a true family. As things stood, he'd taken off, and Mom was involved with a new guy. Maybe if that relationship fizzled out, she might find the time to call me back.

Christian, on the other hand, had changed his phone number entirely and, as of yet, he hadn't shared the new one with his parents. Ginny, a trusted friend of his, had his new number. She was also the center of all gossip in our old town. If anything happened with the Carters, she would give Christian the heads-up.

Eventually he'd contact them. He could be dutiful. He could also be stubborn.

Case in point—his having decided he was in love with me.

I couldn't dissuade him. Couldn't cajole him. Couldn't do anything to veer him off this course of action.

Admittedly, I wasn't trying very hard. Regular hand jobs, blow jobs, and sleeping together? Pretty fucking sweet. Especially the no-strings part.

Of course there are strings. There are always strings. You're using him and that's bad. The time will come when you'll have to pay the piper.

Sure...but that was something I could worry about down the road.

As I directed Christian to drive to the homes of my new clients, I caught a glimpse of his profile. Strong jaw, high cheekbones. Eyes the color of dark moss. Objectively, the guy was damn handsome. And not once, in the last twenty years, had I thought he might be gay or that he might be interested in me romantically. I'd just never gone there. Had never had to because he was always by my side.

In all these years, we'd never had a true fight. We'd disagreed on a few things during the intervening time, but never anything major. Never anything that couldn't be easily remedied with a serious conversation and a meeting of the minds.

Until Leroy.

I'm glad he took the pictures. Even though that was illegal. I'm grateful he cared enough to get me out of that toxic relationship. Only now could I admit that Leroy hadn't been treating me all that well. And, because of my low self-esteem, I hadn't thought to demand more. Hell, I hadn't demanded monogamy because I'd understood that to be a given.

More fool me.

"I said *is that all the houses*? Are you okay?" Christian had parked us on the side of the road and was gazing at me.

"I'm sorry."

His brow furrowed. "For what? I'm happy to drive you around so you'll know what the houses—"

"I'm sorry I got mad about you taking the photos."

"Ah." He nodded slowly. "Know that I didn't want to. I honestly felt I had no other choice."

"How did you know?" That point had been niggling at me for a while.

"One day you told me he was working, but I saw his car in the parking lot of your building. I swear I wasn't snooping. I'd gone out to buy ice cream treats for everyone in the office and on my way back, I spotted Leroy's car." He rubbed his face. "I risked the ice cream melting, but I parked and went to your apartment. Remember you gave me the spare key?"

"You didn't go in." My chest seized.

"Nope. But I used the building key to get me to your place and then I knocked really loudly."

"Oh." This didn't sound like the mild-mannered Christian I knew. "And?"

"He shouted to just leave the parcel."

"What parcel?"

"That was my thought. I knocked again and said something about having left my phone at your place and needing it."

"You'd never—"

"Yeah, but you think he'd know that? He always looked down on me."

That stung...because I hadn't realized.

"He opened the door in his jeans—unzipped—and said he didn't have a clue, hadn't seen it, now wasn't a good time, and could I come back later?"

"Oh." I stared out the windshield. I had a vaguely uneasy feeling we might be watched. And that I was a Black man in a nice SUV. Having Christian at the wheel alleviated some of my concern—but not all of it. "Maybe we can head back?"

"Sure." He started the SUV and pulled back onto the road.

"How'd you know he wasn't alone?"

Christian wrinkled his nose. "He reeked of sex. I mean, I think he'd taken a bath in cum."

I burst out laughing—totally inappropriate, but there it was. "I thought you'd said you've never had sex."

"I haven't." He sniffed indignantly. "But even I know what cum smells like. He just...sweaty sex."

"Sweaty sex can be good."

"Not when you're cheating on your clueless partner." He made a left turn onto the main road that would take us back to Foggy Basin.

"*Clueless partner...*"

"Oh God, Noah, that sounds so bad." He winced, all while keeping his eyes on the road.

"You've always been a straight shooter, Christian. You call it like it is. I should've trusted you. Should've listened to you." Maybe trusted myself as well, but that time had come and gone.

"I tried to tell you that night, but you wouldn't listen. I did quite a few ice cream runs over the next two weeks. When I saw him at home during the day again...I took a chance."

"You climbed a tree and took photographs illegally." I said the words dryly, but—now with more than three weeks of that knowledge under my belt—I wasn't so upset. More worried that he'd done something so risky just to show me what a creepoid Leroy was. We did *not* agree to an open relationship, and I sure as shit hadn't known he was fucking other men in our bed while I'd been at work. "You could've gotten hurt. You could've gotten arrested."

"Sure. But you honestly think Leroy would have pressed charges? Had those photos admitted into evidence? I had an entire bird-watching story made up—but I never needed to use it."

I sighed. "If not for that, we'd still be back there. I'm happier now than I've ever been, so I can't say I regret what you did."

Slowly, the corners of his mouth turned up. He really did have the most beautiful smile. "I'm glad to hear that. Truly."

The next few miles passed in silence as we gazed over the farmers' fields. I could guess at crops, but I certainly couldn't identify them in the blur as we sped by. The abundance of healthy food wasn't lost on me—Christian brought home my favorites from the grocery store all the time. *Employee discount.* I wasn't certain if that was a thing—I didn't know his boss well enough—but I was the happy recipient. And felt guilty at those who didn't have enough to eat. Who couldn't afford the good stuff. "Do you think we should start our own garden?"

"Huh?" He chanced a quick glance my way before refocusing on the road. "What are you talking about?"

"There's that raised flower bed in the back—the one that's almost impossible for dogs to jump up on. What if we tried planting some fruits and vegetables?"

"I don't see why not. Maybe figure out what's there now? I can't remember what's in bloom. I mean, do we want to pull up pretty flowers to plant healthy food?"

"That's a weird question."

"Yes, but they're not our flower beds to pull up."

I snapped my fingers. "Right. Fair point."

"But we can see if there's another patch of earth where we can plant. We'd have to put up a good fence—not just to keep the dogs out, but the rabbits as well."

"We don't have rabbits."

"Nope. Well, not domesticated ones. I spotted a pair near the back of the property line the other day when I was walking Stormy and the pups. Stormy didn't react, but your two barked their little heads off. I have to say, the rabbits didn't look all that intimidated."

"Probably because they can outrun *our* little demons." *If I make him take ownership too, then it won't be as easy to leave me...right?*

Manipulative as hell, but I was getting desperate. "Watch your speed—don't want to get a ticket from Sheriff West."

"That's true." He eased off the gas a little. "I can run the dogs out. What are your plans for this evening?"

"Well..." An idea popped into my head that wouldn't be suppressed. "I'll surprise you."

He grinned. "Sure. I can't wait."

Chapter Fifteen

Christian

Stormy and Sable peed quickly, but River was taking his damn time about finding the *perfect* spot. He wasn't yet in the habit of lifting his leg—something I definitely planned to ask Noah about—so he squatted just like Sable. Tonight? Three times he came super close but then, at the last minute, changed his mind. "Come on, pee already."

Stormy gazed up at me as if to say, *what can you do about these crazy puppies?* I'd discovered early on that she did pee on command—which was greatly appreciated. She'd also done a damn good job babysitting as everyone had been excited when we got home, but not in a panicked way. I'd asked Noah what he thought about us getting a nanny camera and he'd grinned. Said he would pick one up the next time he went to the pet store.

Finally, River squatted and peed his little heart out. He was all grins as I led them back inside.

Noah was there with tiny pieces of baby carrots for them.

All three munched away happily.

He moved into my space.

Our gazes met.

"It's been a lovely night—and we're not dating—but can I kiss you?"

My heart stuttered before restarting at a much faster rhythm. I'd only been fantasizing about this moment for oh, a dozen years. "Uh, yeah, that would be okay. I mean, that would be nice. I mean, you know, whatever you want to—"

He went up on his toes and pressed his lips to mine.

I angled my head down so that he could put his feet flat on the floor again. I wrapped my arms around his waist even as he threaded his hands around my neck and tugged me closer. His mouth was insistent against mine, and I opened for him. He thrust his tongue into my mouth, and I tasted mint toothpaste. *Oh God, he had this planned out. Probably a good thing it took the dog so long to pee. Go River! Wait. The man you love is finally kissing you and all you can think about is your dog? Are you nuts?*

Quite possibly.

No, I'd say probably.

I was also sinking further into the glorious sensation of being held so tightly. He might just have his arms around my neck, but he plastered himself against me and, after a moment, I realized his erection was pressing insistently against my hip. *Well, we'll just have to do something about that.* I was about to offer a blow job when he pulled back.

"We're not dating...but I was wondering if you want a tour of my bedroom, and we can take things further?"

Interesting. I've seen his bedroom. I've slept in his...oh damn. Damn, damn, damn. I cleared my throat. "Further would be completely acceptable."

He grasped my hand and clicked his tongue.

Three puppies gazed up at him.

"Upstairs." He met Stormy's gaze. "My room."

She woofed and headed out.

River and Sable followed her. They almost always followed her. *Helpful that she's a good dog and not leading them astray.* Anything was possible in the future, of course, but for now, she made a great older sister.

Noah tugged on my hand, then flipped off the kitchen light as we passed the entrance. He didn't look back as he said, "I'm not sure you should be so trusting."

"If you're a serial killer, Noah, I figure you'd have offed me long before now." I said the words in jest, but I understood what he was saying.

Don't fall in love with me—I'm a bad bet.

Except he wasn't. He was a great bet. He was loyal and honest and would take care of me in a way no one ever had.

Still, when we arrived at the entrance to his bedroom, he hesitated.

I turned him to face me. "What?"

"I'm nervous."

"Okay." I held his gaze. "Why?"

"Because—" He gestured. "Because I've never done this before."

"Never had sex? Because I'm pretty sure—"

"I've never made love to a guy...like you."

Ah. "Well, I've never made love to a guy like you. So I guess we're even."

"Christian—"

"Nope. You don't get to do that. You don't get to kiss the heck out of me and then throw up barriers." I tugged him toward me, pulling him into my embrace.

He came easily—yielding to me and molding himself against me.

I bent to kiss him.

He kissed back with fervor. He thrust his tongue into my mouth with a clear plan to dominate.

Letting him take over the kiss was as easy as breathing. He had a forceful personality that turned me on. That I appreciated. I was okay with yielding. With giving up control. On the other hand, if he ever asked me to take the reins, I certainly would—I'd do whatever he asked of me. Always had and always would.

He pulled back from the kiss. "Too many clothes."

I chuckled. "That's true."

We'd dressed in chinos and shirts to visit Miss Esmeralda and to go to the nice restaurant.

He stood back and started unbuttoning his white shirt—such a contrast to his dark skin.

Mirroring him, I unbuttoned my pale-blue shirt. They were abandoned on my chair as we started working on our pants. Somehow, we'd wound up in my room, even though he'd asked me to join him in his.

Our three pooches had followed us in here and were now snoozing—with River sleeping with Sable in her bed. Their closeness was what I wanted with Noah. Someone to always rely on. Someone who would have my back. He'd always done those things when we'd only been best friends—I worried I might lose that if this lovers thing didn't work out.

I shucked my pants, and next came the boxer briefs.

Noah did the same, and I was able to see his lovely erection. We hadn't discussed position, but I knew I'd be bottoming tonight. And maybe all nights—if we repeated this.

He hesitated.

I cocked my head.

"Supplies."

I grinned. "Stopped by the drugstore on the way home, one night last week. All good."

"I like you being prepared."

"I was a boy scout."

He laughed. "That you were. I never did anything like that."

"Because you were busy with your dogs and cats. You had way more important things going on in your life."

Another smile. "And now I'm rebuilding my menagerie."

I grasped my erection and stroked myself. Unless this was a long and necessary tangent, I wanted to keep us moving forward.

"We'll talk about rescuing a cat. Right now, though, I want you on the bed."

"Yep." I sort of squeaked that. Then I hustled to my bed. I pulled the duvet and top sheet down, then lay in the middle of the bed with my head propped on a pillow.

He gave himself a couple of good tugs. Then he moved to my nightstand—rightly intuiting where I'd left the supplies. He pulled out the bottle of lube—and removed the safety seal. Then he opened the condom box and pulled out a long length containing several.

"Optimistic?"

"Oh, we'll see how you do. Depending on how things go, I might let you fuck me. We're off work tomorrow."

"I remember. You don't have any clients?"

He shook his head. "I like the idea of being off work at the same time as you."

To me, I heard a very intimate statement there—that coordinating our schedules mattered because he wanted to maximize our time together. That meant something. *Who are you kidding...that means everything.* Yet I held myself still as he donned a condom. Then he put one knee on the bed and the other and headed my way.

I spread my thighs.

He settled between them. He lubed his finger.

My cock curved toward my belly, but I shifted my balls out of the way so he'd have unfettered access. I'd do whatever it took to keep him close to me.

He ran his fingers around the outside of my hole.

The cool liquid against my skin provided an interesting contrast. "I'm ready, Noah. Hell, I have been for about half of my life."

"And I never knew." Slowly, he sank one finger into me.

Since this was a new sensation for me, I tried to lean into it. He wasn't hurting me, that was for certain. "More. Please."

He grinned that mischievous and wicked grin I found so endearing. Then he added another finger.

Again, a strange sensation.

"Have to make certain you're ready for my cock. You're awfully tight."

"Never done this before." I ensured my breathing was slow and steady.

"Well, we're just going to have to change that." He scissored his fingers over and over—loosening me for him. Then he twisted his wrist and thrust his fingers in farther.

I was barely adjusting to that sensation, when he touched part of me that lit a spark and sent electricity arcing through my body. "What the hell...?"

"Prostate." He eyed me. "You really have never done this."

"I lived with my parents and was one hundred percent celibate. So when would I have had—"

He brushed it again.

My eyes rolled back in my head as the pleasure overwhelmed me.

"Look at me, Christian." Said in a strong tone of voice.

I obeyed his command.

"I'm going to introduce you to so many things. I have toys. I intend to use them on you. If you're okay with that."

The final sentence appeared to be an afterthought, but I was totally fine with that because I was, in fact, fine with anything he proposed. He'd never hurt me...but he might introduce me to all kinds of fun things. I knew about my prostate, of course. Just had never gone on an exploration mission. Now I was glad of two things—that he'd introduced me to it and, more importantly that it had been him and not some random hookup or a complete stranger.

He withdrew his fingers.

I moaned in protest.

He grinned as he lubed his cock. "I'll make this good for you, I promise.

"I believe you." I pulled my lower lip through my teeth. "I'll always trust you."

His eyes shadowed for just a moment. "I don't know if I'm deserving of that trust—but I'll definitely never abuse it." He leaned over to lick a drop of precum from the tip of my shaft. "You ready?"

"Been ready for about thirteen years."

He chuckled. "Never saw that. Not sure I'll forgive myself for not noticing."

Before I could respond, though, he lined his cock up with my entrance.

I grasped the sheets.

He pressed in ever so slowly. Barely a whisper, at first, but then with some insistence.

It hurt. I'd known it might—but knowing and enduring were two very different things.

Sweat broke out across his brow as he continued to press into me. "This is the worst of it. Once—" He let out a groan.

Something changed with me. Because the head of his cock was in? Perhaps. I was a little more naïve than I liked.

He held my gaze. "I'm going to move now."

I nodded.

Slowly he pulled back a bit. Then he pressed forward. Back. Forward. Inch by inch.

The burn eased and a strange and intense pressure fell in behind it. I'd read accounts of this, and they were fairly accurate. I'd disregarded the ones that shouted about how good the first time felt. I'd also skimmed the horror stories. Knowing Noah would take care of me meant those things wouldn't happen. I was certain of that.

"I'm bottomed out. Do you know what that means?"

I nodded. "That you can't go in more."

"And how do you feel?"

"Strange...?"

"Perfectly normal. Now, you can ask me to stop at any time. I should've said that before—"

"But you didn't need to because I already knew. Make love to me, Noah. Show me how good it can feel."

He grinned. "Yeah, I can do that."

And he proceeded to.

Chapter Sixteen

Noah

While apparently Christian had spent half his short life imagining this moment, I'd had a couple of days. Since the first blow job, I'd tried to picture what this instant might look like. Might feel like. Even what it might smell like.

Whatever I'd thought, it paled in comparison to reality.

His flushed chest, neck, and face. His rapid breathing. The smell of sex and sweat.

For me? The tightness and heat from him. The unwavering trust emanating from him to me that overwhelmed. I hadn't imagined it would be like this. That the emotional would be enough to break me wide open. To melt the ice around my heart. Because I could see now, in a way I'd never been able to before, that I'd never given myself completely to anyone—not even Leroy.

As I withdrew almost to the tip, then slid back, the realization hit me.

I can love this man.

Hell, I do love this man.

In that *way.*

I wanted to shout it, but Christian wouldn't believe me. He'd think this was a sex thing—and so I'd just have to find other ways to show him.

Withdraw.

Thrust.

Pull out almost to the tip.

Push home again.

Only to no home I'd ever known. Even through our panted, mingled breaths something shifted.

"Noah."

I refocused my attention. Back into this moment. I snagged his erect cock and tugged to the rhythm I set. "I need you to come, baby. Okay?" Because I was on the verge, and rarely did I come before my partners. I'd always focus on their pleasure.

"Yes." He hissed out the word even as he came in my hand, spurting cum everywhere.

I tried to nurse him through the orgasm, even as I came myself. I went rigid, held still, and let the climax wash over me. Envelop me. Send me soaring above the earth in the most mind-shattering orgasm I'd ever had. Why? Why with him? Why now?

Because you've never had this connection with someone before. Because this is what true love feels like.

I'd told Leroy I'd loved him—had believed that. Folly. Bullshit. I'd thought if I said it, then I could manifest it. Turned out, if someone else manifested it, it might've just rubbed off on me. I collapsed on top of Christian.

He was a solid guy, and he held me close.

I rested my cheek on his sternum and listened to the pounding of his heart. I'd no doubt in my mind that he'd enjoyed this as much as I had.

"That was…" He let out a long exhalation.

I tilted my head so I could meet his gaze. "Yeah?"

He blinked repeatedly, then a tear slid down his temple and into his burnished gold-and-auburn-colored hair.

"Don't cry." I levered myself so I could roll off him and pull him—admittedly awkwardly—into my arms.

He hiccupped as another tear rolled down.

I pressed a kiss to his temple, tasting the salty residue of the now-flowing tears. I didn't know how to stem them—I didn't have the words. I was certain this wasn't a physical thing—he'd had pleasure. No, this was emotional…the one thing I was no good at.

He blew out a breath. "I don't mean to cry. I just—" He sniffed. "—I'm so glad I waited, Noah. That you were the first. And I know it didn't mean to you what it meant to me—"

I placed my index finger on his lips. "Hush. You don't know what it meant to me because I haven't shared. It means everything, Christian. I can honestly say I've never connected with someone like that before. And I don't know what this means—it's too raw." I smiled. "I'm going to clean us up, then tuck you in for the night."

"You'll stay?"

"Of course I'll stay." I kissed him soundly. Then I carefully removed the condom and knotted it off. I rolled off the bed and headed to the bathroom.

Huh.

I put the condom in the trash and then put the trash can on the counter. No way was I leaving it anywhere the dogs might get into it.

If you get tested, then you could go bareback.

Well, fuck me. I got tested regularly—smart thing to do. But I'd never considered going bareback with anyone.

Anyone.

Not even Leroy—which probably should've been my first hint that I never fully trusted him.

Christian? One hundred percent. If I asked him to commit to me, he'd do it. And if I committed to him, I'd do it. But what would that mean for our friendship? I wet a washcloth as hot as I could stand and washed his cum off my stomach and chest. Then I rinsed it out and headed back into his bedroom.

His eyes were closed.

I washed him carefully, ensuring he was as clean as I could get him. The damage appeared to have been confined to our chests, so we didn't have a wet spot to worry about. I returned to the bathroom, pissed, then headed back to bed. Since Christian appeared to already be asleep, I tucked myself in next to him and drifted off as well.

Morning came as a rude awakening as Stormy leapt onto the bed and began licking my face. Only a sliver of light came through the blinds. Apparently, the dogs weren't going to wait for full morning. "I'll go."

Christian stretched. "I'll start breakfast. Eggs and toast or pancakes?"

For the first time in as long as I could remember, I was damn hungry in the morning. "Pancakes?"

He pressed a kiss to my cheek. "You've got it."

I dressed in jeans and a henley and gave Christian one wistful look as I hustled the dogs down the stairs, through the kitchen, and out the back door. All three headed for the fresh grass and squatted.

Watching them, I chuckled. "Sorry guys. My bad."

Stormy woofed. When she was done, she loped over to the far side of the run.

She sniffed the ground with determined focus—which made me curious. So, I ambled over with two ruffians nipping at my heels.

"Did you find something good?" I stepped close to Stormy, but still gave her space. She was already a big dog, but she'd yet to grow into her paws—that were massive.

She continued to sniff the ground.

River and Sable joined in.

I chuckled as the morning dew sank into my bare feet.

Christian.

We made love last night.

He's...my forever person.

I had no doubt in my mind. The only thing left was to show him how I felt. To prove I wasn't just reacting this way because of the sex.

That said, the sex had been pretty epic.

I'd never made love to a virgin before. He was so very different from everyone who had come before. The thing was...I had known lots of good men back home. But I'd always picked losers.

Christian had patiently sat back and waited for me to get my head out of my ass. If he hadn't sent those photographs of Leroy and the faceless man he'd been fucking, then I would still be living seeped in the lie—thinking I was happy. Telling myself Leroy loved me. Living the fantasy that we'd...

Fuck.

I didn't know Christian's dreams. I'd gone along with everyone else believing he'd marry Laura, eventually take over the reins of the factory, and they'd have kids, maybe a dog, and a nice, big house.

Never, in a million years, had I considered that might not happen.

Then Laura'd run away.

I...figured Christian would find another nice woman and marry her...? I'd been arrogant when we first arrived in Foggy Basin. I figured I could find a nice woman for him to date and eventually marry—even though I didn't want to be alone. Even then my subconscious had recognized that for the first time in my life, I was living with someone who loved me. Platonically, of course. But his willingness to literally pack his belongings in an SUV and follow me across the country showed a devotion I didn't deserve.

Now I understood he was also running from his demons. From his family's expectations. From the town who would forever see him as the man left high and dry when his fiancée left town with another man.

A close call for all of them.

Would Christian have continued the charade? Married a woman he might care for, but with whom he'd never have a truly fulfilling relationship? Much like I'd gone along with Leroy. If I'd had niggling doubts, I'd shoved them so far down that I still couldn't find them.

"Breakfast!"

I turned to see Christian standing on the back porch, waving a spatula.

Sheesh, how long have I been out here navel gazing?

My feet were frozen, Stormy had finally stopped sniffing that special spot, and the other puppies were each trying to eat the other's ear.

I whistled and started striding for the house.

No one followed.

I spun to make eye contact with each of the dogs. "Breakfast. Food."

Stormy bolted, and the other two, clearly watching her, followed.

I chuckled as I held the door open for them.

Christian was putting a platter of pancakes on the table.

Real Canadian maple syrup, blueberry jam, and two mugs of coffee sat waiting as well. Before that, though, I had something important to do.

I snagged him around the waist and pulled him in for a long, deep kiss.

He molded himself against me—ensuring there wasn't a whisper's distance.

I wrapped my arms around his neck and held tight.

His hands traveled down my sides, along my flanks, then down to my ass where he squeezed. He pulled me even tighter against him, pressing his erection against my hip.

I pulled back. "The pancakes will get cold."

"That's what the microwave's for." He grinned.

"Are you sore?"

He shook his head. "You were gentle, Noah. Which I appreciated."

After a moment, I nodded. He wasn't wrong—I'd gone easy with him. And would continue to until he was more accustomed to this. Or until he asked me for more. "You could always make love to me..."

He kissed my nose. "You bet. But you're right—food first. Plus, don't you have to go to the pet store?"

"I do." I did a little awkward shrug. "And I might be dropping by to see Pam at the shelter."

"Make certain you buy everything you need for the cat. Or cats. I'll feline-proof the yellow bedroom."

I arched an eyebrow.

"Remove all the breakables and anything that isn't washable in case there are accidents. I should probably talk to Miss Esmeralda at some point about where we should be putting things. She said the attic and the basement, but we might run out of room. I mean, we might end up buying stuff of our own."

"True. No rush, though. As long as we take care of her things, we're okay until I've got more money coming in. Oh, Pam said I could bring some flyers and business cards, so that's good. I'll check out the rec center over in Hartsville as well. Anywhere I might drum up business."

He pressed a hand to my cheek. "I'm so proud of you. Now—eat."

Stormy woofed.

"Okay, feed the dogs first and then eating."

He grinned. "Works for me."

And so we did. Then I left an hour later to get through my long list of tasks so I could get back to Christian as quickly as I could.

Chapter Seventeen

Christian

M iss Esmeralda was in exceptionally high spirits when I arrived. I'd thought to maybe drop by, but she'd actually called me and had asked me to show up at eleven o'clock on the nose.

Just before the appointed time, I crated the dogs and headed to the nursing home. I found my landlady in the sitting room with an older, distinguished gentleman sitting beside her. *Has she found a gentleman caller? He's a bit younger than her...but go, Miss Esmeralda!*

She beckoned me to sit in a high-backed chair across from her. "This is Mr. Sampson."

I extended my hand in greeting. "Christian Carter."

The man had a strong shake—but not overpowering. Just solid. He eyed me with incisive dark-brown eyes that somehow suited his shock of short, white hair.

What will Noah look like when he goes gray? Will I be around to see it?

I retook my seat.

"Mr. Sampson is my lawyer." Miss Esmeralda sat a little straighter.

"Ah." *Is she kicking us out? We could probably find another place to live...right? Hopefully she gives us enough—* I was so absorbed in my panic, that I almost missed her next words. "I'm sorry, can you repeat that?"

She gave her lawyer a knowing smile. "Told you he'd be shocked."

Mr. Sampson regarded me. "Miss Stanton has asked me to draw up the papers so that, after her death, you and Mr. Gainey inherit her house and property."

My eyes widened. "No. No, no, no." I turned to the woman I was coming to think of as a friend. "You can't do that. Surely you have family—"

"Only child of only children. I have a few distant cousins who never responded to my letters about thirty or forty years ago. Look, if I don't bequeath the house to someone, the state might take it and, if they can't find someone, they might keep the profits. I love California, but not enough to hand them a pile of money. I knew from the moment we spoke on the phone that you were the one. The only question is whether I give it to you alone or whether I include your, uh, best friend."

I chuckled to myself. She missed nothing. "I can't speak for Noah. I don't want to tie him to me. That said, he loves the property." If I didn't spend all my savings, I would have enough for a down-payment on a little property of my own. Dillon paid me a living wage, so I'd be okay. Noah could keep the house and... I blinked. How would we split the dogs? And what if I fell in love with the cats? Were we going to have a custody arrangement? Because as happy as he'd been this morning, my worries that I wasn't enough for him continued to crowd my mind.

"You have time to decide whether you want to accept this gift." Mr. Sampson offered what I thought of as a sympathetic smile. "This is a lot to take in."

I blinked. "I met Miss Esmeralda yesterday."

Slowly, the lawyer nodded. "Yet she spoke to me last week. She wants things settled."

"She can change her mind, right? If she meets someone else who she thinks would be better suited—"

"There is no one better suited." She narrowed her eyes at me. "I see you as an intelligent young man."

"Well, okay—"

"I'm offering you a chance to secure your future—and your friend's." She pointed. "You probably don't think I know, but I do. You talk a lot when you don't realize it. That first night? You told me your life story."

"Did I?" I had a vague recollection of a three-hour call. Noah and I had been on the road for about twelve hours, and I'd been ready to collapse. But I'd promised Noah I'd find us the perfect rental—and I had. "I didn't intend to."

She pursed her lips. "You being left at the altar was a blessing."

"I wasn't really at the altar—"

"And you being in love with someone who you thought would never return that affection made me sad."

"I didn't mean to say all that—"

"But then the two of you came by yesterday, and I saw such love—going both ways. Certainly, you might not work out as a couple."

"I'm not sure we even qualify as a couple—"

"You'll make it, though. I feel it in my bones. And if you don't, then one of you can hire Mr. Sampson, and one of you can hire Mrs. Estwick—a very competent attorney—and you can sort out the assets. The point is, that you'll both come away with something." She patted her hair. "As opposed to the state."

I blinked. "And there's truly no one else?"

"Mr. Sampson says I'm not supposed to leave him anything. Something about solicitor/client relationships."

"It might appear I coerced you and, although I appreciate the sentiment, I'm quite comfortable."

Miss Esmeralda eyed me. "You could give him a tip once everything's done. Another reason for me to leave you everything."

"Of course." When Mr. Sampson wasn't around, I'd get her to tell me a more specific dollar amount rather than just *a tip*.

Which meant I was going to go along with this harebrained scheme. "Let me discuss this with Noah. If he agrees, we'll...do whatever you need."

Miss Esmeralda grinned. "I knew you were a smart young man." She pointed to Mr. Sampson. "He'll bring me the paperwork, and we'll get this going. I might die tonight."

My gaze shot to Mr. Sampson.

Who gave me a little shake of the head. No, he didn't know anything specific.

I grasped Miss Esmeralda's hand. "You have to stay alive for a long time, okay? Are we clear?"

She pressed her hand to my cheek. "For you, my dear boy, I will try."

About ten minutes later, I was driving around Foggy Basin aimlessly—trying to figure out how I was going to explain this to Noah.

In the end, I headed home. I always wanted to be home when I wasn't working. Dillon was a great boss, and I loved interacting with the patrons, but what I really needed was to be home with Noah and our little family of pooches. He'd said he was looking at some rescue cats, so cat-proofing the spare bedroom needed to be a priority.

After I ran the dogs out, let them do their business, and then did a bit of basic training stuff—which Stormy aced while Sable and River...well, they tried. Anyway, I gave them each a sliver of freeze-dried salmon and then I led the pile of pooches upstairs. I wondered if they might go into my room, but they eagerly followed me into the yellow room. Bright and sunny. *Will cats care about that? Oh well, I will. Noah will. That's what counts.*

I removed the beautiful quilt and folded it gently. I put it in the linen closet and grabbed an older blanket that was fraying around the edges. I laid that on the bed and then set about putting all the breakables in a hope chest that sat at the end of the bed. *God, I hope they don't scratch this.* I had the impression Miss Esmeralda wouldn't care—especially if it meant we were giving a home to some rescue cats.

Through our conversation that first night—which I still held so dear—she'd made it clear she loved animals and had, when she was more mobile, had a variety of pets in the house. Her last dog passed twelve years ago, with the final cat passing three years ago. She'd made it clear that if our dogs or cats caused damage, that she only asked we *put things to right however you see fit.*

She wants to gift us this house? This land? That doesn't seem real. That's not how things work in real life. Except they just might. If I were in her shoes, I'd pick the best people with the biggest hearts. Noah certainly fit that description to a *T.* He always put people—and animals—first. Probably why he'd chosen so many guys who weren't right—he'd thought he could *fix* them. *Is that how he sees me? As someone who needs to be fixed?* I tried to be independent. And reliable.

And strong. But sometimes I wasn't, and I worried he might just see me as another wayward soul in need of assistance.

As I wrapped a china figurine in a lovely lace doily, something caught my eye. Gently, I lifted the picture frame and turned it over. A moment passed before I realized what I was looking at.

Esmeralda, clearly, wearing a white- or cream-lace dress. My first instinct was a wedding dress, but I didn't think so. Her long, black hair appeared windswept—as if someone had turned on a wind machine. The woman next to her wore overalls and some kind of a checked shirt. I couldn't discern the colors because the photograph was black and white. A random guess was red and black or perhaps red and blue. Was this the Lucinda whom Esmeralda had mentioned yesterday?

They gazed at the photographer—Lucinda with a solemn expression, while Esmeralda sported a small smile. A knowing smile. As if saying, *I have a secret none of you know about, and I'm not going to share.*

Or perhaps that was fanciful thinking on my part.

Standing mere inches apart, they appeared close—although whether from physical proximity or some intimacy that wasn't readily visible, I wasn't certain.

I placed the framed photo on the bed. I'd take it to her. She might get upset, of course, or seeing it might make her smile. My gut instinct was smile. If she hadn't wanted it around, then she would've tossed it years ago.

After completing the task of cat-proofing the room as best I could, I took the photograph downstairs. I wrapped it in newspaper and tucked it by the front door—making a mental note to show it to Noah before putting it in my SUV so I wouldn't forget I had it.

Time to eat. And maybe start dinner. I had some nice chicken breasts. I also had some fresh mushrooms and some string beans. Or maybe tacos. Tacos were Noah's favorite. I had a taco kit with crunchy shells as well as some ground beef. Somehow, I figured I could make a meal.

I eyed the three dogs who'd dutifully followed me down the stairs. "Playtime?"

Stormy woofed.

The other two looked confused.

I led them into the family room, where I plopped down onto the floor. All at once, I had three dogs trying to climb over me, kiss me, and generally attempt to get my full attention. I hugged, gave scritches, and generally had a great time.

My life can't get any better than this.

Well, Noah could tell me he loved me in a romantic way. But I wasn't going to try for the moon when things on earth, at least for today, were pretty darn sweet.

Chapter Eighteen

Noah

"Snowy and Jasmine couldn't have found a better home." Pam grinned as she tucked the paperwork away and gazed at the two cats in the crate I just happened to have brought with me.

I'd completed the application online for the siblings. Because I'd rescued from Safe Haven before, Pam had approved me right away. They were also getting fuller. In fact, a mama cat and her seven kittens had just been rescued from a hoarder—along with eleven other cats. I wanted to take mama and babies, however I'd managed to suppress the urge. The family required constant care, and between my own brood, Christian, and my burgeoning business, I had too much going on.

Plus, Snowy and Jasmine—seven- and nine-year-old cats respectively, had been in the shelter for a while and really needed a forever home. Something Christian and I could absolutely offer.

I waved, then hefted the crate as I headed out. Neither cat was particularly huge, but their combined weight—along with the crate—was pretty heavy.

At the pet store, I grabbed a cart to put their crate in. The temperature outside was already warm, and the temperature inside the car would climb precipitously. I wasn't going to risk them getting heatstroke.

As I stepped inside, Sam waved. "Hey, you're back."

"Yep." I pointed to the crate. "And about to spend some serious dough."

The gorgeous man clapped his hands. "Can't wait." The twinkle in his eye assured me that although he'd be happy for the sale, that wasn't the only reason he did what he did. No, labor of love more likely. He gestured to the crate. "May I?"

"Absolutely." I stood back as he made his way over.

"Their names?"

"Snowy and Jasmine."

He chuckled. "Let me guess—the white Himalayan is Snowy. Is she a seal lynx point?"

I was impressed. The light tan stripes along the cat's face and the color of her paws were pale enough to almost go unnoticed. "She is. She used to be a queen, but she retired last year. Jasmine was just a plain domestic shorthair who lived in the house as well. The owner got sick earlier this year, and her medical bills are horrendous. She couldn't keep the cats and so surrendered them as a pair."

"And now you're rescuing them." Sam placed a gentle hand on my arm. "That's so good of you."

For a moment, I simply started at my arm. His dark skin was a shade lighter than mine. The pads of his fingers were rough—clearly he was a man who worked with his hands. He was just the sort of guy I'd have chosen in my previous life. He appeared nice, though, so that was a bit different. Not someone I had to try to change. "Uh, maybe can you show me to the cat aisle?"

"Sure. And I can help you pick out what you need."

"Oh, as much as I appreciate that, I'll be okay."

"Really? I offer a discount to anyone who rescues an animal from Safe Haven."

In that moment, I didn't know whether to call *bullshit* or not. No question, he was hitting on me. The question was whether or not I wanted to be wooed by a stranger. A really cute, and apparently nice stranger, but I guy I didn't know all that well.

Still, a discount was a discount, and even a few dollars helped—I could buy more stuff for the cats as well as a couple of squeaky toys for the dogs. I'd likely regret that decision when I wanted to get frisky with Christian—

Christian.

Huh.

By the time I had everything loaded in the car—with Sam's help, I was tired. I just wanted to get home, get the cats settled, and maybe take a nap.

Preferably with Christian in my arms.

Christian's never really had anything of his own in his life—he's always been living for other's expectations. Whether marrying Laura, working for the family business, or just continuing to live at home—those were all things he did for other people. Hell, moving to Foggy Basin was something he did for me.

So what did Christian really want in life? Was he really happy to settle with me and my growing menagerie? Could he spend the rest of his life working at a grocery store and be happy? Would it all be enough, or would he one day walk out the door like my father had?

Ouch. Christian is nothing like your father. If he got a woman pregnant, he would never abandon her. Just like he's never going to abandon you...unless you send him away.

Or unless he met someone else.

That thought turned my stomach into knots. I didn't want him to find anyone else. I wanted what we had to be everything he'd ever wanted. Everything that would bring him joy.

All I ever wanted was for someone to love me—and now I had that. Someone who would love me for me. Who would accept my collection of stray pets and help rather than be disdainful.

Really, at the end of the day, I just wanted someone who would be here for me. Someone who wasn't going to quit, or cheat, or do a runner on me after just a few months.

Certainly, I hadn't picked a single partner who fit that description. And my mother hadn't chosen a single man to be my stepfather who was a tenth of the man Christian was. At some point, I'd probably have to examine why Mom and I continued to make such bad choices. Because plenty of good men were out there—of all races—yet she and I had both fallen into a pattern of picking assholes who treated us badly and then, as often as not, walked out the door on us.

She deserved better.

I deserved better.

Doing something about her situation was damn near impossible. She was an adult—living her own life in a destructive way. I doubted very much I could get through to her.

But Christian, in his own way, had finally gotten through to me. That realization might've only come after more pain—I'd never forget seeing those pictures of Leroy—but from that bitterness had risen something beautiful. Something incredibly special. My best friend had found the courage to tell me how he felt. He'd laid his heart on the line.

I hadn't rejected him—but I hadn't embraced him either. How many times had I said *we're not dating, but*... And then proceeded to do something that people who were dating might do? I wouldn't blame Christian if he were confused.

You love him. You've always loved him—just in a different way. But now? The physical intimacy is nice, but you want more. You need more. You deserve more. So hurry the fuck along and tell him how you really feel.

The miles passed, and I fought the urge to put my foot to the floor. I didn't want one of Sheriff West's deputies pulling me over. Aside from the ticket I'd have to pay, I would also be later getting home to see Christian. I doubted he'd found someone else today, but I needed him to know *right fucking now* how I really felt about him.

I pulled up to the gate, hopped out and opened it, then drove to the house. I jogged back to lock the gate and, by the time I got back to the car, Stormy and the puppies were doing their best to stick their noses in the crate. "Be patient." I met Christian's gaze. "I love you."

"I know. I love you too. I was going to bake some chicken—very healthy—but I opted for tacos instead."

"My favorite."

"I know." He gave me that sly smile.

I pulled him into my arms and kissed him soundly.

He molded himself against me.

We eagerly fought for dominance with the kiss. In the end, though, he let me win.

Finally, I pulled back. I met those beautiful green eyes and stared into them. "I love you. I mean, I really love you. I didn't know what love was, but you've shown me every day for the last twenty years. I know I'm a little late to the party—you figured out the romantic love thing about, what...?"

"Thirteen years ago. Give or take."

I blinked. "You're a patient man, Christian Carter."

"You're worth the wait, Noah Gainey." He placed a quick chaste kiss to my lips. "The cat room is ready, so how about you introduce me to the newest members of the family and, after we get them settled, we eat tacos? Then I want to take you and the dogs out for a treat."

I cocked my eyebrow. "A treat?"

"You'll have to wait and see."

Since I trusted him, I snagged his hand and brought it to my lips so I could kiss it. "Yes. Whatever you want."

His eyes lit. "Great! Now...cats...?"

"Snowy and Jasmine."

"Snowy and Stormy...well, life will never be boring."

"Probably not." I hefted the crate.

Christian grabbed the cloth bag with their toys and treats. With the other hand, he grabbed their large bag of food. "I'll come back for the litter and the other bag."

"It's got the bowls and a few more things. I bought a cat tree, but we'll have to take your SUV to get it."

"We should consider swapping vehicles." He followed me into the house and up the stairs—with our three dogs hard on our heels. Once he put everything he carried on the floor, he whistled and had three pooches dutifully following him.

I shut the door. "Okay, ladies, this is your new home." I almost opened the crate, then decided to keep it shut until Christian returned with the last of the things. While I waited, I sorted through the bag and got the food organized.

He was back within just a few minutes. He put the litter box and bag of litter on the ground, then handed me the bag with the dishes.

"I'm going to put our lovely pooches downstairs in the family room so the cats aren't scared out of their wits."

After grabbing the three squeaky toys, I handed them to Christian. "Hopefully they'll all enjoy and not try to steal."

He eyed me.

I sighed. "Yeah, we'll wait until after dinner."

"Well...I have plans for us for after dinner."

"Oh?"

"Yep. Food first, treat later."

"Treat?" I cocked my head.

He wagged his finger. "Let me dish out dinner while you finish in here." He placed himself before the crate—out of reach of any claws.

As I expected, none appeared.

"They're adorable, Noah. Perfect additions to the family."

"You mean, purrfect." I elongated the *r*.

He rolled his eyes. "If everyone gets along, do you see them roaming the house?"

"I worry about Miss Esmeralda's things."

"Tomorrow I'll tackle cat-proofing the rest of the house."

After a slight hesitation, entirely mine, I pressed a kiss to Christian's cheek. "Thank you."

His cheeks turned a cute pink shade. "I want this too, Noah. We need to create our own menagerie. Our own family." With that, he left, clicking his tongue, and with three dogs obediently following.

As I set out the litter box, and organized the food—on a desk that was easily accessible for the cats, but that even Stormy couldn't reach—I tried to see our lives ahead of us. Would Christian still want me as time went on? Conversely, what if I got tired of him?

Even as I had the thought, my mind rebelled. Sam had flirted with me, and I hadn't been the least bit interested. Before, he'd have totally been my type—except maybe too nice—but that was hard to tell after just a couple of meetings.

The point was—I had someone who professed to love me. Someone I could see loving in return.

I opened the crate.

As predicted, Snowy exited first. I'd guessed she'd be the braver of the two.

Jasmine, not to be outdone, soon followed.

Snowy leapt off the bed and headed to the litter box. She went inside, did her business, and then jumped out. Eyeing her food, she leapt back onto the bed and then to the desk where she dug into the wet food I'd put out.

Jasmine, having watched her sister with great interest, leapt onto the desk and started in on her food as well.

"I'll drop in after dinner to check up on you and as well when I get home from...wherever. Try not to destroy everything." I placed a small blanket in their crate and put the two beds on the human bed. One was an enclosure and one was just a big basket. Both had enough room for the two cats—should they choose to share.

"Dinner's ready." Christian's voice carried through the closed door.

I eyed the cats. Snowy had finished her wet food and was eyeing the dry kibble. Clearly having decided that could wait, she leapt onto the bed and started nosing around the various beds I'd set out for them. She decided on the enclosure. She settled in and started licking her paw.

By the time I turned my attention back to Jasmine, she'd finished her food, nibbled on a couple of pieces of kibble, and met my gaze with her intense eyes.

"You'll be happy here, I promise."

She leapt down and headed over to the litter box.

I waited until she finished, then watched her as she leapt onto the bed. She made a beeline for her sister, and nestled herself into the enclosure as well.

Snowy grasped Jasmine's head and started licking her ear.

Both cats purred so loudly, I could hear them—despite being several feet away.

They'll be okay.

Maybe I will as well.

I headed down for dinner.

Chapter Nineteen

Christian

F oggy's Creamery was like an old-fashioned ice cream parlor, and I had to say McClain was a kind and gentle soul who appeared to have Noah and me nailed—a young couple in love. That seemed to amuse the man with gray hairs at his temples. Maybe even touched his heart? I couldn't be certain.

Judging by how Noah demolished his ice cream—well, I did as well—we were definitely going to be coming back repeatedly.

After tossing our napkins into the recycling bin, we headed a nice park. I held Stormy's leash while Noah had Sable's and River's. He snagged my hand. "This is nice."

"It's a beautiful evening—not too hot and not too cold." *Yeah, like that's not a super lame thing to say.*

"It's going to be super hot in the summer."

"And we might have some snow in the winter. So quite similar to back home."

"Do you miss home?"

"Hmm?" I'd been eyeing a bench and hadn't caught his quietly spoken words.

"Do you miss home? Do you have any regrets?"

"Nope. None. Want to sit on the bench or keep walking? Walking's good for the dogs—might tire them out."

"Tomorrow we'll try—one at a time—to introduce them to the cats." Noah smiled. "Stormy lived with several at Paxton's farm."

"Snowy and Jasmine are about the same size as the puppies." I eyed the two who alternated tugging and then needing to be coaxed. They apparently still weren't sold on the whole *walking* thing.

"Bench would be nice." Noah headed in that direction, with me beside him.

We settled quickly—each dog receiving a morsel of kibble for their good *stay*. Whether that would last was entirely up in the air. The puppies had the attention spans of goldfish, and Stormy had spotted a squirrel and was on full alert. If the puppies spotted the rodent, chaos might ensue.

Noah squeezed my hand. "Was the treat the creamery? Because that was a good choice."

"I know, right? That was awesome. We definitely need to come several times a month." I wasn't certain if Noah might make a joke, or even just a comment, about putting on weight. He didn't—and I was glad. He was perfect just the way he was. "Uh, no. I went to see Miss Esmeralda today."

"Again? So soon?"

"She asked me to drop by. I wanted to sort of get a sense of where she was on us adding to the menagerie. If she was adamantly opposed, I would've contacted you."

He met my gaze. "But she was okay with it."

"More than okay. Noah—" I took a deep breath, knowing the next few moments were going to be so critical to our relationship. "—she wants to leave us the house."

His eyes widened.

"She had her lawyer with her. If you're okay with this, he'll prepare the paperwork in both our names. If you don't want the hassle, he can just do me."

"I'm sorry, I thought you said she wanted us to have the house...?"

"And all the property. I didn't dare ask how much that totaled. I mean, it doesn't really matter, because I don't plan to sell the place. Which means..." I met and held his gaze. *Please understand why I'm going to say what I'm going to say...* "—well, if you're thinking of selling in the next few years, I'd rather you not put yourself on the deed. I can pay you rent every month—"

"On a house you own?"

"Well, I don't want you to feel like I'm not being fair to you."

He pressed a hand to his forehead.

This isn't good. Not going the way I'd hoped it might.

"Are you writing the obituary to our relationship two days after it started?"

"Uh...no...?"

"Then why wouldn't I put myself on the deed? Let's take money off the table for a moment."

I wasn't certain that was possible, but I was willing to try.

He met my gaze. "Are we a forever thing? Be honest."

"For me, that's an absolutely *yes*. I've been in love with you since we were five. Physically attracted to you for over a dozen years now. So, this isn't new for me. Imagining how our lives would play out—"

"Tell me." Again, with those intense dark-brown eyes.

"You. Me. Dogs, cats, and maybe a bird or two. A menagerie. Living in a home and being happy. Maybe, I don't know, we might consider kids. Or not. Our pets can be our kids. The most important part is that it's you and me—together." I let out a breath as I'd said the words in a rush. I inhaled and exhaled again. "Can I see us in Esmeralda's house? Yep, I can. I found a picture, that I'll show you later, of her and another woman. I'm pretty sure they were lovers—back when they couldn't really be. But you and me? We can hold hands in a park. I can tell my boss I'm gay, and he'll be pretty okay with it. Our vet is gay and so are some of your clients. Foggy Basin is everything you promised—and more." I squeezed his hand. "But I don't want to tie you down."

"And if I want to be tied down?"

I held my breath.

"You came to this town knowing nothing about it. All you knew was that I wanted to be here. So you went along with this harebrained scheme—"

"No regrets, Noah."

He gave me that *I'm speaking now and it's damn important* look.

I nodded.

"And now you've laid your heart on the line. You let me see how you've felt all along. This is easy for you—in some ways. You've always wanted this, and now it's within your reach."

"Yes."

"You asked me what I wanted—after I'd seen those pictures of my boyfriend fucking another man."

I winced.

"No, you were right. I mean, illegal, but we'll let that go."

I nodded.

"All I saw was that I needed to get away. This town seemed as good a place as any to start again."

"Okay."

"I knew starting Tips, Tricks, and Back Flips would be tough. But I also knew I had you beside me. With you beside me, I can do anything."

My gaze swept over our contented dogs—all three of whom were sleeping. "You can do anything. You don't need me."

"Maybe. Possibly. Probably." He pursed his lips. "But why would I go through life alone when I have the most amazing man beside me? He's offering his heart, soul, and body. He wants to take care of me and, in turn, will have to learn to let me take care of him."

This time, I pursed my lips. No one had ever taken care of me. I didn't know what this might entail.

"A partnership."

"Yes."

"A love affair."

My heart soared. "That's what I see. If you don't, though—"

He pressed a finger to my lips. "But I do. I see what you're offering, and I want that too."

"Oh."

He chuckled. "Yeah. *Oh.*"

"What..." I cleared my throat. "What do we do? Do I contact Miss Esmeralda and let her know it'll be the two of us?"

"Do you want this to be a forever thing?"

"Yes. No hesitation. Yes." I held his gaze, begging him to respond.

"Well, it's that way for me as well. Let's go into this thinking it's a *until death do us part* thing."

The tightness in my chest loosened. "Yes. That. I want that." I leaned toward him.

He met me halfway.

We sealed the bargain with a kiss.

Chaste, of course, because a couple had just entered the park. Two men with two kids in a stroller and a dog on the leash.

The dog spotted us and bolted.

Clearly surprised, the guy let go of the leash.

In a flash, Noah handed me the leashes for River and Sable. He leapt up and put himself between the charging poodle and our babies.

The poodle, clearly not expecting this, tried to back up.

Noah caught the leash.

The one man jogged up. "I'm so sorry about that. She caught me off-guard. She's strong and stubborn."

"No worries." Noah handed over the leash. "I'm Noah, and this is my partner, Christian."

Partner. I loved it.

I was so wrapped up in that thought, that I missed the rest of the introductions.

Stormy was tugging at the leash.

"You're a dog trainer?" The taller man grinned. "I think we might just hire you."

And just like that, all was right in the world.

Epilogue

Noah

The sun shone brightly on our wedding day.

Quite fitting we were marrying in the pasture of our property. Our home.

Dillon had volunteered to bring Miss Esmeralda, and she surveyed her former land with clear appreciation. We'd shown her pictures of the changes we made, and she would always grin. She'd decided to give the property before she passed—so she wasn't making us wait to do what we wanted. We still paid her a monthly sum to help offset her expenses, although she still had quite a pile of money in the bank. Or so she'd shared with us. Mr. Sampson believed in complete honesty. He was a good man.

She was an even better woman.

Christian had found the courage to bring the photo of Miss Esmeralda and her *best friend*, Lucinda.

Miss Esmeralda had teared up, then told us about the woman she'd loved more than life herself and how they'd been *roommates* until Lucinda died in 1988. Miss Esmeralda had been alone all this time, clinging to the belief she would one day join her true love.

That's devotion.

The same as I have for Christian.

He and I held hands as we walked down the sort of makeshift aisle. We'd invited all my clients—numbering well over a hundred, as I'd been busy in the last eight months. Many had declined, but a good number were here today.

Malcolm, who was standing up for Christian, stood tall next to the celebrant—with a shit-eating grin on his face.

Soren was standing up for me, and he was grinning pretty hard as well.

No one from back home was here. Christian had sent a cable to his parents, letting them know.

Turned out, about six months ago, Laura had returned with her husband—pregnant with twins and desperately wanting her mother. The Frankstons, desirous of avoiding a scandal again, gifted twenty percent of the factory back to Christian's parents. The split was six-ty/forty. Which meant that no matter how irresponsible his parents might be in their personal lives, the factory would be protected. They'd made it clear they weren't interested in acknowledging a gay son and would be just fine if he stayed in Foggy Basin and never returned home.

My mother had sent the silver set she'd inherited from her grand-mother—more sentimentality than I expected. That gift marginally changed my opinion of her. Right until she said she couldn't make the wedding because her new husband was taking her to Tallahassee.

Put her out of your mind.

I claimed to Christian that didn't care. He didn't appear convinced, but he'd have to trust me on that.

He handed Stormy's leash to Malcolm while I handed Sable's and River's to Soren. His Tibby was being cared for by Janelle. Her Roxy was in training to be a therapy dog and showed great potential.

Christian took my hands and gazed into my eyes.

The service passed in a blur.

As we kissed, River barked excitedly—something he always did. A touch annoying at certain critical moments—but absolutely adorable today.

Soren gripped me tightly when offering his congratulations. "I just knew it."

I chuckled, while swallowing back the tears of happiness. "You and Malcolm called it correctly."

"Did someone say I was right?" Malcolm was there to embrace me while Soren grabbed Christian in a bear hug.

Christian giggled. "You were right. From the start, you were right."

"Music to my ears." Soren glanced toward Sam. "And who is he?"

"I take it you'd like an introduction?"

"Uh—" Soren cleared his throat. "If it's not too much trouble."

Christian laughed. "It's not. I was jealous when I first met him—thinking he might have designs on Noah."

"He did." I snagged him by the waist, twisting the leashes. "But by then I knew you were the one for me." I turned my attention to Soren. "His name is Sam, and I'm happy to make introductions."

"If it's not too much trouble. Oh, I better snag Tibby from Janelle." He paused. "Although I have to say, Miss Esmeralda appears quite smitten with my lab."

"She's thrilled to have us living here." I beamed. "The care home loves that Stormy's now a qualified therapy dog. Her visits are the highlights of Miss Esmeralda's week."

And I knew I was right. I'd done the training of Christian and Stormy, but they'd had to pass the certification without me. And they had. First try. I was pretty damn proud of that.

Stormy nuzzled Christian's hand. "Oh, right. I think she has to go. Do you want me to take them as well?" He gestured to Sable and River.

I shook my head. "I'll come with you."

Our guests had been organized haphazardly, and clearly no one was waiting for us to make our way down the makeshift aisle. In fact, dogs were sniffing each other and enjoying themselves—which was always the point of today.

Letting Stormy guide us, we headed off to a quiet corner of the field.

As she peed, I pressed himself against Christian, tucking my head under his chin. My favorite spot.

He held on tight. "Best day ever?"

"Yeah, actually, it is." I angled my head back so our gazes could meet. "We have guests to feed."

He glanced over. "Actually, Malcolm, Soren, and Dillon seem to have things in hand." We had food for the guests and treats for the dogs. Everything carefully labeled because of allergies.

"I'm thinking—" I cleared my throat.

"Thinking...?"

"About expanding our family." My heart sped up. We'd said we weren't going to do anything different in our lives until we were married. *Am I ready for this? What if he says no?*

"Expanding...?" He squeaked that.

"Kids. Foster kids or our own kids...however that might look."

He grinned. "I think that's a fantastic idea."

My expression lightened. "Yeah?" I didn't tease him. Now wasn't the moment.

"We'll see what we need to do—"

"I have the papers in my desk."

His eyebrows shot up. "Yeah?"

I nodded.

"Well then, tonight, we'll sit down and look them over." He pressed a kiss to my temple. "You okay?"

"I am now." I met his gaze. "I'm sorry I didn't see it before, except if I had, and I hadn't had all those crummy relationships, then I wouldn't appreciate what I have now. I've got the best of both worlds."

He cocked his head in question.

"My best friend *and* my husband. That's pretty damn perfect." I pressed a kiss to his lips.

A kiss he returned eagerly because hell, yes, this was damn perfect.

Thank you for reading Christian and Noah's story!

Want more Gabbi Grey?

Check out her Love in Mission City series, set in beautiful British Columbia.

The first book is

Ginger Snapping All the Way (Love in Mission City Book 1)

Also available:

Stanley's Christmas Redemption(Love in Mission City Book 2)

The Beauty of the Beast (Love in Mission City Book 2.5)

Sleigh Bells and Second Chances (Love in Mission City Book 3)

A Daddy for Christmas 2: Foster (Love in Mission City Book 3.5)

Rayne's Return (Love in Mission City Book 4)

Gideon's Gratitude (Love in Mission City Book 5)

Love in Mission City: The Boyfriend Gamble

Love in Mission City: The Four Seasons

Love in Mission City: The Boyfriends Duet

Love in Mission City: The Shorts

Rayne Check

Archer's Awakening

Leo's Lust

Puppy Pride

A Daddy for Christmas 3: Lorcan

Thought You Were the One

Love Without Reservations

Page Against the Machine

The Lightkeeper's Love Affair

Ace's Place

Marcus's Cadence

Not in it for the Money

Also:

Axe to Grind

Grindstone's Edge

Voice to Raise

Hugh (Single Dads of Gaynor Beach)

Anthony (Single Dads of Gaynor Beach)

Xavier (Single Dads of Gaynor Beach)

Love Furever (Friends of Gaynor Beach Animal Rescue)

Husky Love (Friends of Gaynor Beach Animal Rescue)

Yorkie to My Heart (Friends of Gaynor Beach Animal Rescue)

A Furever Home (co-written with Kaje Harper – Friends of Gaynor
Beach Animal Rescue)

My Past, Your Future

If Only for Today

Catch a Tiger by the Tail

Solstice Surprise

Valentino in Vancouver

You See Me

Sun, Surf, and Surprises

Ginger in the City

Caressa's Homecoming (Bound by Love Book 1)

Cole's Reckoning (Bound by Love Book 2)

An Uncommon Gentleman

A Sensible Gentleman

Didn't See You Coming

Hot Rucking Canadian

Big Rucking Disaster

Unlocked and Unlost

Audiobooks

Ginger Snapping All the Way

Stanley's Christmas Redemption

Sleigh Bells and Second Chances

Rayne's Return

Gideon's Gratitude

Rayne Check

Archer's Awakening

Thought You Were the One

Love in Mission City: The Shorts

Page Against the Machine

The Lightkeeper's Love Affair

Ace's Place

Marcus's Cadence

Not in it for the Money

Hugh (Single Dads of Gaynor Beach)

Anthony (Single Dads of Gaynor Beach)

Love Furever (Friends of Gaynor Beach Animal Rescue)

Husky Love (Friends of Gaynor Beach Animal Rescue)

My Past, Your Future

If Only for Today

Catch a Tiger by the Tail

Solstice Surprise

An Uncommon Gentleman

A Sensible Gentleman

Didn't See You Coming

Want a free short story? The story is set in Gaynor Beach, California where there are plenty of single dads and puppy rescues! You can sign up for my newsletter so you can keep up with all the great stuff I'm doing as well as pictures of my own pooches, Ally and Finnegan.

Hemingway's Happy Day

Love contemporary MF romances? What's better than love in the beautiful Cedar Valley in British Columbia, Canada? Find small town romances with a touch of angst, a bit of heat, and a lot of heart...

The Absolution of Abigail Reardon (prequel)

The Luminosity of Loriana Harper (Book 1)

The Making of Marnie Jones (Book 2)
The Redemption of Remy St. Claire (Book 3)

Interested in knowing more about Gabbi?

Sign up for her newsletter

Follow her on Bookbub

Follow her on Instagram

USA Today Bestselling author Gabbi Grey lives in beautiful British Columbia where her fur baby chin-poo keeps her safe from the nasty neighborhood squirrels. Working for the government by day, she spends her early mornings writing contemporary, gay, sweet, and dark erotic BDSM romances. While she firmly believes in happy endings, she also believes in making her characters suffer before finding their true love. She also writes m/f romances as Gabbi Black and Gabbi Powell.

www.ingramcontent.com/pod-product-compliance
Lightning Source LLC
Chambersburg PA
CBHW021009180626
46814CB00003B/1203